# Refugee 87

# Refugee 87

### Ele Fountain

**LB**

LITTLE, BROWN AND COMPANY
New York Boston

Quotation from *Sean O'Casey Plays 1* by Sean O'Casey ã Faber and Faber Ltd.;
Ebook rights granted by kind permission of the Estate of Sean O'Casey.

Cover design by Sammy Yuen. Texture photograph © Coffee krai/iStock.com
Ship photograph © B-D-S Piotr Marcinski/Shutterstock.com
Ocean photograph © Andrey Polivanov/Shutterstock.com
Boy photograph © Ronald Summers/Shutterstock.com

Little, Brown and Company
Hachette Book Group
1290 Avenue of the Americas, New York, NY 10104
Visit us at LBYR.com

Originally published in 2018 by Pushkin Press in Great Britain
First U.S. Edition: June 2019

Little, Brown and Company is a division of Hachette Book Group, Inc.
The Little, Brown name and logo are trademarks of Hachette Book Group, Inc.

The publisher is not responsible for websites (or their content) that are not owned by the publisher.

Library of Congress Cataloging-in-Publication Data
Names: Fountain, Ele, author.
Title: Refugee 87 / Ele Fountain.
Other titles: Boy 87 | Refugee eighty-seven
Description: First U.S. edition. | New York; Boston: Little, Brown and Company, 2019. | "Originally published in 2018 by Pushkin Press in Great Britain." | Summary: In the Middle East, fourteen-year-old Shif and his best friend Bini embark on a continent-crossing journey of survival after they are imprisoned and become refugees.
Identifiers: LCCN 2018029973 | ISBN 9780316423038 (hardcover) | ISBN 9780316423014 (pbk.) | ISBN 9780316423007 (ebk.) | ISBN 9780316423021 (library edition ebk.)
Subjects: | CYAC: Prisoners—Fiction. | Refugees—Fiction. | Survival—Fiction. | Best friends—Fiction. | Friendship—Fiction. | Middle East—Fiction.
Classification: LCC PZ7.1.F6785 Re 2019 | DDC [Fic]—dc23
LC record available at https://lccn.loc.gov/2018029973

ISBNs: 978-0-316-42303-8 (hardcover), 978-0-316-42300-7 (ebook)

Printed in the United States of America

LSC-C

10 9 8 7 6 5 4 3 2 1

*For Lily and Scarlet*

When it was dark,
you always carried the sun
in your hand for me.

—Sean O'Casey, *Red Roses for Me*

# Boat

Cold salty water stings my eyes and soaks my T-shirt. I cling to the clammy wooden edge of the boat as a huge wave swells toward me. The boat tips, and I gasp as people slide against me and the air is pressed from my chest.

The sky is turning from light to dark gray; white foam tops the waves. The wind pushes relentlessly against my face, and with the next rolling wave the boat dips so low that buckets of water gush in over the side, soaking me again with freezing water. I feel it creeping above my ankles. No one cries out. Even the baby strapped to the mother beside me is quiet.

Green-gray waves make a wall around us. We rise to the top of another but there is nothing to see except spray blowing like rain in the icy wind. Europe is sprawled somewhere in front of us but I can't see land. As we slide into the trough, more water rushes over the side of the boat. It's up to my knees. My feet are numb but I can tell that my shoes are heavy with water. I look up again and see a swirling wave bigger than the others rolling toward us in fury. The boat tips. This time we keep on tipping. The wave crashes over us as if we are on the shore, only we're in the middle of the sea. I hear screaming and then nothing as water rushes over my head.

I can't tell which way is up to sky and wind, and which way is down toward the depths of sea beneath. I open my eyes. They sting but show me nothing more than cloudy bubbling water and the legs of someone just out of reach. I kick up once, my chest burning. I kick up again, knowing that in a second I'll no longer be able to fight the desperate urge to breathe in. I kick one last time, my legs tingling. I am about to pass out just as wind blasts my face; I suck in air and some spray.

Choking, I pant and gasp; the currents tug me left and right as the swell lifts me up and down. I cannot swim but instinct makes me kick my feet to stay afloat. The shoes my mother bought with three weeks' wages are so heavy. I try to push them off without going under.

I know I can't kick water for long. Already my thighs and arms feel tired. I see four, maybe five, other heads swirling in the waves. How can three hundred people disappear so quickly?

A yellow plastic bag washes toward me. There are clothes inside. The knot has been tied tightly so the bag is like a floating pocket of air. I cling to it.

A boy appears next to me, bobbing up from under the waves like I did seconds before. I reach out my hand to him. He looks at me. His eyes are big and oval-shaped and he reminds me of Bini, my best friend at home. I reach my hand out to him again and he tries to grab it but instead sinks beneath the waves. He doesn't come back up.

Who will come to save me? Who knows where I am apart from the others tossing and bobbing in the waves like me? What would Bini do now?

# Before

# Best Friend

T he square root can also be written as a fractional exponent."

"Yes, Bini. Next time raise your hand first."

I'm pretty smart, but Bini is smarter. I can't tell if our math teacher is proud of us or just irritated by us. Maybe both. We know as much as he does now. Ato Hayat keeps a university textbook in his drawer and copies homework questions for us from it. It came with a sheet of answers, and it's fine if we get the solutions right, but if we get them wrong, he snaps at us that knowledge is a gift and we should study harder. He doesn't understand the questions or the answers.

I'm going to be an engineer. Bini has wanted to be a doctor for as long as I can remember. When we were really small, he would make me lie on the floor so he could listen to my heart beating, or my liver— he wasn't quite sure back then. As we got older, he started asking random questions, like "Where does sweat come from?" Or "Why does your heart keep on beating and not just stop when you go to sleep?" I didn't know the answers and I didn't really care.

He would say, "Just think of all those things your body does that you don't understand, but *you* want to go and learn about how to build a bridge." Usually, I'm not fast enough to think of a clever reply until it's too late to sound clever anymore. Saying "Yeah, but how would a doctor reach a patient if there was no bridge to drive over?" seems a bit lame twenty-four hours later. Still, we are best friends. Maybe because we like to argue with each other.

# Normal Day

The school bell rings, and even though I'm only heading to the market we race to the gate.

"See if you can get there first for once, squirt," Bini yells over his shoulder.

All the boys in our class were a similar height until summer term, then suddenly Bini was a bit taller, and now his body can't seem to stop shooting upward. I fix my eyes on his back, dodging the other kids in their blue uniforms, hopping on and off the dusty curb as I weave around bodies and jump clear of oncoming cars. I see the market up ahead. People and small piles of vegetables spill from the sidewalk onto the street. Next to some open sacks of cinnamon, Bini is leaning against a jacaranda tree, mouth closed, pretending that he isn't out of breath even though I can see his chest heaving up and down.

"Not bad," he says, smiling, "for a squirt."

I punch him on his skinny arm.

We wander home beneath a solid blue sky, the hot sun baking everything it touches. Our houses are next door to each other, in the middle of a low, flat-roofed terrace on the edge of the city. Inside there is no upstairs, just two rooms crammed with everything we need. We sleep, eat, cook, and do homework in these two rooms. Quite often it feels as if we spend so much time in each other's houses we might as well just knock a big hole through the wall and put a door there. When I was seven, we were going to move somewhere bigger, but then my father died and we had no more money—only what Mom earns mending and making clothes at the workshop two streets away.

I don't remember Dad being ill. Apparently there was nothing the doctors could do. One day he went into the hospital, and he never came back. Bini's dad moved out at around the same time. He went to find a better job on the other side of the city. Our moms became very close. Mom says that money isn't everything. We are lucky to have a roof over our heads and it doesn't matter what that roof is made of or how big the house is underneath it. Sometimes I wish I had my own room, though.

We step around the little kids sitting on the curb. Too young for school, but not too young to look after the five goats eating grass at the shady edge of the road.

Bini and I sprint the last few yards to our front doors. I hurry to the wooden cupboard in the corner of the living room, take out a faded red T-shirt and jeans, and change out of my uniform.

Seconds later, I hear Bini knocking. How does he get changed so fast? Before I've properly opened the door, he pushes in, schoolbooks piled in his arms.

"Let's get this done quickly, then we'll have more time for me to beat you at chess."

"Is time all you need? You should have said so before," I tease.

The only gift I have from my father is the chess set he made for my sixth birthday. The board is a tin tray and the pieces are carved out of wood—carved by him. It's my most precious possession. Not least because chess is the one thing I can always beat Bini at and it drives him crazy. We will keep playing until one day he wins, and I will never be able to beat him again after that.

# Something Weird

The next morning, Mom leaves before I do. Work is busy right now, which is good and bad. My little sister, Lemlem, whines as she is bundled out of the house. I hear Mom promising her something nice as the door clicks shut behind them.

Two minutes later, Bini knocks. I grab my bag and we walk down the road to school, Bini slowly, me at a normal pace to keep up with his giraffe strides. As we get closer to school, the roads are wider and the houses bigger. We're about to turn the final corner when Bini slows down.

13

An army truck is parked about a hundred yards from the school entrance. Four soldiers sit in the back, rifles on their knees, watching the schoolkids pass in front. I look ahead to the gates. No one is kicking a ball around outside. The other kids are filing into school without looking up. One mother turns around and starts walking back the other way, taking her sons with her.

"What's going on?" I ask Bini.

"No idea," he replies.

We keep quiet as we pass the truck.

Our first lesson is chemistry. Ato Dawit is my favorite teacher, but today I don't enjoy the lesson. Ato Dawit seems tired. No one raises their hand to answer questions.

At lunchtime Bini and I head for our normal spot over by the shady trees in the corner of the yard.

As we start to eat, I watch Kidane walk slowly in our direction with two of his friends. There isn't any more space to sit down, so I wonder what he wants. My stomach does a little flip. Kidane had the same growth rush as Bini, only he grew wider as well as taller. Now he looks about four years older than the rest of our class. A class Bini and I have been moved up to only because of our good grades.

"Why is the army hanging around outside our school today?" asks Kidane.

"How should we know?" Bini answers.

"Perhaps you should go home and ask your dad." He looks first at Bini, then at me.

Bini stares at him. "Why don't you go and ask your dad? Or would you need to help him with a big word like *army*?"

Kidane grabs Bini by the collar of his school shirt. "At least mine hasn't run away. It's people like you and your dad who make it dangerous for the rest of us," he hisses.

Bini stands up. Kidane is still holding his T-shirt, but now their eyes are level. Bini doesn't flinch. Kidane shoves him backward and walks away with his friends, glancing back to give us both a death stare.

My mouth feels dry when I speak. "What do you think he meant when he said we make it dangerous for the rest of them?"

Bini is frowning at the ground, deep in thought. "I don't know, but I feel like everyone else does."

"Have you heard anything from your dad?"

"No. He hasn't sent Mom any money, either. She says it takes time to find a job that earns enough." He pauses. "Six years seems long enough, though."

"Kidane must know my dad died," I say.

"He's an idiot," says Bini. "That's one thing I am sure about."

After school, we head home in silence, Bini kicking at stones. I almost feel like letting him win at chess but decide he'll feel better soon enough. Instead I let him reach check.

# Police

As dusk approaches, Bini heads home for dinner. Mom and Lemlem still aren't back. This means Mom is finishing a big order. Maybe a wedding dress or something for a government official. Lemlem won't start school for another year so she spends most days, or at least part of the day, at the tailor, too, playing in the scraps, picking cotton from the floor, and helping fold fabric.

My stomach growls, but there is no bag of injera hanging from the cupboard door ready for dinner. I know that nearly everywhere will have sold out of it by now. The tsebhi won't be enough on its own.

I'm not supposed to leave the house after dark. I count to twenty, but there's still no sound of footsteps approaching, so I decide that dusk doesn't count and take five nakfa from the old milk-powder tin.

I head down the empty road to the nearest shop. The light is still on.

"Kemay amsikum, Solomon," I call.

He stops putting tins on the shelf and turns around. "Kemay amsika."

I point to the flat round basket on the counter containing whatever injera is left. Two pieces. Solomon takes my coins and stuffs the injera in a bag.

The sudden rumble of a vehicle approaching startles me. There is hardly ever much traffic after dark, especially out of the city center. I turn but am momentarily blind to the dark road, an imprint of the shop's lightbulb still white in my eyes. My vision clears and I see an army truck and the silhouettes of three soldiers with rifles jumping down from the back. Their heavy boots crunch in the sandy gravel of the road. I turn quickly back to the bright shop, not wanting to attract attention. I hear one of the soldiers knock on the door of a house next to the truck. The other two are at a house two or three doors farther away.

I take the bag of injera and walk back in the direction of my house.

I hear a raised voice from inside one of the houses, then a second deep voice shouting, "Hey. Hey!"

I instinctively know this shout is directed at me. I haven't done anything wrong, but everyone avoids the military. I break into a run, skidding as I turn the corner to my street. I can hear heavy boots crunching quickly down the road I just turned off. I fumble for a key in the folds of my pocket. Using two hands, I guide it into the lock, stumble inside, then push the green metal door back to click shut as quietly as my sweaty hands will allow.

I sit very still. I realize that I'm holding my breath and try not to pant. Each breath sounds loud, like a betrayal. Outside the door it is silent.

I'm not sure how long I sit like this. Perhaps twenty minutes later, there is a muffled thud as the front door eases open. I freeze. Then my mother's voice filters through the panic.

"Shif, what are you doing sitting there in the dark? What happened?"

Lemlem runs over and hugs my knee. "What happened?" She mimics my mother.

"I went to buy injera," I say in a voice that doesn't feel like my own. "Some soldiers went into the houses next to Solomon's shop. I think they were looking for someone. Then they shouted after me, too, so I ran. I don't know if they saw which house I went into—I didn't turn around."

My mother's hand has moved involuntarily to her mouth. She is completely still.

Lemlem smiles up at me, then turns to look at my mother. "Mom?" she asks.

As if emerging from a trance, my mother begins to issue instructions. "Lemlem, can you fetch some water, shikorina?" Then, looking back at me: "Why did you go out after dark? We have some bread in the tin, which would have been enough. Do you not listen to me?"

"I'm sorry, Mom." I shrug. "I didn't check it."

"I need to know where you are when I'm at work.

If I can't trust you at home on your own, then perhaps you will have to come and stay with me in the shop."

I get up from the floor. "I've been coming home on my own for six years. Now you want to treat me like a little kid?" I'm beginning to feel that maybe I should be the one who's annoyed here.

"You don't let me go to other friends' houses if they invite me. I always have to be at home so you know where I am." Someone in my chemistry class is arranging a trip to the movies this weekend, and I wasn't even going to ask Mom if I can go, because I know what the answer will be. "Isn't it okay to just walk down the street? I'm not eight anymore."

She seems to calm down a little and picks up the bag of injera from where I left it on the floor. "Tomorrow is your big test—am I right? You should get some good rest tonight. I'm going to get dinner ready."

My mother prepares the food with the same energy she used to tell me off. It's as if she's afraid to be still, in case something bad happens within the space she has created. While she prepares dinner, I finish a game of gebeta with Lemlem and let her win.

Mom talks about the beautiful dress she's been working on and I run through matrix formulas in my head, nodding every time she looks over and says, "Don't you think?"

Finally, when Lemlem is sleeping, I sit next to Mom and ask quietly, "Why is it okay for me to hang out with Bini, but not okay if I want to bring other friends home, or go to other friends' houses?"

Mom seems tired now—very tired.

"Shif, you know it's better to have a few close friends you trust. With too many friends, you don't know who else they will talk to, or what they might say about you."

"To who?"

She smooths the fabric of her dress over her knee. "The army has ears everywhere. We don't want to give them any reason whatsoever to take an interest in our family."

"But we've done nothing wrong. Why would they take an interest in us?"

"Tonight you gave them a reason. You ran away from a soldier and now he will be wondering why. He didn't see where you went, but do you think he won't come back? The more you go out or bring friends back, the more people will talk about us. They will say that you're often out, say that strangers visit our house. People will say anything to deflect trouble from themselves, but they often don't have very much imagination. Don't give them anything for their imagination to work on."

"The government can't put everyone in jail. If they put everyone in jail, then who will be left to spy on?"

"We can talk about this, Shif, but not now. Tonight you need your sleep. You have to get good grades on your math test."

She knows I get nothing but good grades in math. But I can tell that the conversation is over before it has even begun. Again.

I can be patient. I've been patient for a long time.

# Test

With a slight flutter in my stomach, which may be the math test or may be the stale bread I had for breakfast, I knock on Bini's door. No answer. Weird. He normally gets to our house first while I'm still getting ready.

I can't be late today so I start walking slowly down the road, knowing that with his long legs Bini will catch up with me in a few minutes. I'll hear the crunch of his shoes as he runs down the sidewalk after me, and lurch forward as he slaps me on the back when he could just as easily say hello.

Twenty minutes later, I arrive outside the school alone. I realize it's the first time I've walked to school on my own this year. I head to my homeroom to go over my notes one last time.

Bini doesn't come to the test.

He doesn't come to school all day.

When classes finish, I walk to the market alone to buy tomatoes and then go home.

No one answers when I knock on Bini's door.

I knock again more loudly and shout, "Bini, it's me!"

As I turn to leave, the door slowly opens and Bini's mother, Saba, looks at me.

"What is it, Shif? Bini's at the market."

"I just wanted to check to be sure he's okay," I answer, confused—I didn't see him at the market. "We had a big math test today and he missed it."

"Bini is okay," she says.

"If he's not sick, then can I come around a bit later? So we can go over the answers?" I add, realizing I sound a bit desperate.

"Don't worry about that," says his mother. "There's no need. Bini won't be coming to school anymore."

She closes the door and I stand very still, wondering whether she will open the door again, laughing at the joke she's played. But Bini's mom isn't the joking type.

# Secret

"How was the test?" Mom asks cheerfully as she walks in with Lemlem.

I look up from my homework. I haven't really done any of it. I can't concentrate. It's as if my brain doesn't come to life without Bini there to irritate me.

"It was mostly easy. Just one question I wasn't sure about."

"I'm sure you will get top marks," she says, kissing me on top of my head.

"Maybe this time I will," I answer.

She looks at me quizzically. She doesn't like it

when I'm not open with her, I realize, even though she's keeping things from me.

I eat dinner mechanically, not thinking about the food in front of me. I am able to think only of Bini's mother's words: *Bini won't be coming to school anymore.* This is a massive deal, yet she seemed unmoved, normal. As if Mom said, *Dinner is ready. Please step over the meteorite that landed in the house—I haven't had a chance to sweep it up.*

We only have to complete this year, then go to military school for two years, then we'll be free to apply to a university, to study whatever we want. Everyone spends two years at military school, but Bini and I have moved up through school so quickly that we'll go early. Going early was exciting when it was Bini and me. I don't want to go on my own. On my own I won't be special; I will be the little kid whose friends are still at regular school.

Anger swells slowly inside me. I can always line my thoughts up like chess pieces waiting for moves. But now all I can think about is how soon Lemlem will go to bed. How soon I can confront my mother. This time I will not let her turn me away with promises of "later."

Eventually, after we have cleaned up by candlelight because there has been another power cut, I hear Lemlem gently snoring on the bed she shares with my mother. Now that the time has come to speak, I can't think of how to frame my questions. As my thoughts sprawl, I look over at my mother sewing a colorful strip of fabric to the edge of a white gabi. Finishing her day's work.

She looks up at me and smiles. "When will they tell you your results?" she asks.

"Next week. Mom, Bini has quit school."

She looks down at her sewing, concentrating, even though I know she could sew with her eyes shut.

"He's top of the class."

She is silent.

I feel the anger grow once more. This time it is sudden, like a flame on paper.

"Why would Saba take him out of school? I mean, is school dangerous now, too?" I think of what Kidane said to us during lunch break yesterday. "Someone at school, one of the other kids, said Bini's dad was dangerous. I think he was talking about Dad, too. Why would he say that? Is there something else I have to be careful about?"

More silence. I can't bear it any longer. "If Dad hadn't died, then perhaps I could have asked him. Perhaps he would have talked to me instead of ignoring me."

I'm almost shouting now and Mom leaps out of her chair and puts her hand over my mouth. Her hand smells of new fabric.

"Don't wake Lemlem," she says softly.

But I know it's not Lemlem she's worried about disturbing. It's our neighbors. Anyone on the street who isn't Bini or his mother, the only people we can trust.

My mother sits back down. I can tell she is organizing her thoughts. Her response will be calm and orderly. The exact opposite of my questions. She will start by telling me that it's part of living in a big city, that she grew up in a village but in big cities you cannot trust people in the same way.

But she doesn't say that.

She says, "Shif, your father isn't dead."

# Truth

It feels as if time has frozen. We stare at each other but my mother's face is blank, impossible to read, the only movement caused by the flickering candlelight.

"There are many things I haven't told you, Shif. But I can see that I have no choice but to tell you now."

I sit. Not next to her, but close enough that her words won't wake Lemlem.

She pauses. "Your father was a lecturer at the university." She momentarily closes her eyes. "He was brilliantly clever. At school he was always top of his class, but there was only ever one thing he wanted to do. He wanted to be a teacher. After military school he started teaching at the university. The kids loved him, and he was very popular with the other staff. Your father always made people feel they could be themselves around him, because that's the way he was around other people." She pauses again. "One day there was a meeting between the teachers and some government officials. They told the teachers that they wanted to know what the government could do to improve teaching standards. Your father suggested that they could be paid more. A man sitting at the back of the meeting asked your father to come outside into the corridor for a moment. No one saw your father again."

"Who was the man?" I ask.

"The man worked for the government. They tricked your father. They tricked everyone in that room. They didn't want to know about how to improve lives for teachers. They wanted to know if there were any teachers at the school who would criticize the government."

"But he only asked if they could get paid more."

"The government pays teachers' wages."

"That doesn't make any sense. Then you could accidentally criticize them about anything. Without even knowing you'd done it."

"Now you're beginning to understand."

"Why take him away? Why not just tell him to be happy with what he's paid?"

"The government had to be sure your father wouldn't make anyone else feel the same. They wanted to make an example of him."

"Make an example of him? But everyone thinks he's dead."

"His friends don't know what happened to him. And that frightens them more."

"So if Dad isn't dead, then where is he?" I can feel hot tears pooling in my eyes.

"There are camps where they send people like Dad. No one knows where they are and no one can visit. Your father cannot leave. He may never leave. I don't know for sure that he is still okay after six years in prison. That's why I told you he's dead."

I feel as if Dad is dying all over again.

"Shif, I didn't tell you these things because not knowing them is safer for you. But I'm learning that you are just like your father. You're not happy with answering questions—you must ask them, too. But for your safety—for our safety—you must understand that you can't."

Lemlem begins to stir.

I wait for a minute, then do exactly what she asked me not to do. "How can this be connected to Bini not going to school?" I ask.

Lemlem opens her eyes.

*"Shhh, shhh,"* Mom soothes her. "It's time you went to bed," she whispers to me. "We've talked enough tonight. We'll talk again tomorrow evening. We'll talk every evening until I've told you everything. I think you realize, Shif, that you must tell no one what I've said tonight."

♟

I lie awake on my hard bed, listening to Lemlem and Mom softly snoring. Everything is as it was last night. But I feel as if a new life has begun tonight. A life with no secrets. As I stare up at the shadowy ceiling, I wonder what Dad is doing now, what kind of room he is sleeping in.

I remember Dad coming home from work one day with a present wrapped in a cloth. My chess set. I step softly toward the cupboard and slide it out. I lay it on my bed and take out the pieces. I look at them, as if I expect them to reveal more. Instead, I feel as if each piece is a connection to my father. They have an energy. My father is alive.

I will not stop asking questions until I know everything. If Mom is right about the dangers that brings, then she will have to keep her promise and tell me herself. Then there will be no need for me to ask other people what is going on.

For the first time ever, I will already know.

# Leave

The next morning, I sit in geography class but cannot concentrate on what the teacher is saying. I realize, too late, that he is talking to me. I look at him blankly.

"Ato Girma, would you mind repeating the question?"

He gives me a stony stare. "Then will you be joining us for the remainder of this lesson?"

I nod as the rest of the class laughs.

I feel as if the words my mother shared with me last night are hovering above my head. My secret is lit up for everyone to see. No one has mentioned the empty seat next to me, Bini's seat. Normally Bini and I would see who could solve an equation the fastest, who could finish his exercises first. Today I want to be invisible, and I want my lessons to end so I can run home and discover the other pieces to the puzzle of my life.

To pass the time, I begin to daydream again. If I want to become the best engineer in the country, I must get top grades in math. But for the first time I begin to wonder if that's what I want. I want to get top grades, of course, but maybe I could do something different. Would I like being a teacher? If I were a math teacher, I could help the smartest kids. Unlike Ato Hayat, I would know how to teach them new things—hard things. Perhaps that's why my father wanted to be a teacher. To help others learn what he already knew. To do it well.

The bell rings for lunch and I head toward the cafeteria. Other kids from my class sit in groups around the edge. I could go over and join them, but I know they won't want to talk about differential calculus. Without Bini, I will have to become self-sufficient. I will need to push myself at school because he won't be there to do it for me.

There is a Bini-shaped hole, threatening to swallow me up.

When the bell rings to mark the end of English, I stuff my things into my backpack and rush to the gate. Maybe the boredom of another day off school has made Bini more desperate to beat me at chess. A small part of me also wonders if Saba will have changed her mind. I push away the thought that something serious must be behind her decision. Something that Mom has promised to explain.

I put the key in the front door and realize that it's already unlocked. I push it open and see my mother sitting on the bed with Lemlem on her lap and Bini's mother next to her. I can see that Mom has been crying.

"Shif, come and sit down," she says without looking up.

As I sit down, Saba hugs Mom and says she will go home to get things ready.

Mom whispers in Lemlem's ear to go sort through the threads in her sewing basket.

"But I want to stay and listen," Lemlem says.

"Find some bright thread and maybe I can sew a pattern on your dress this weekend."

Lemlem hops down and walks eagerly over to the basket in the other room.

As soon as Lemlem has gone, Mom turns to me and says, "Shif, the soldiers you saw two days ago are taking part in a giffa." Reading my mind, she says, "They are rounding up any boys or girls they think are trying to escape military school. Sometimes they have a tip-off; sometimes they just take anyone who looks old enough."

"Why do they need to round people up? I thought everyone just went?"

"Whatever you've been taught about military school, Shif, forget it. Forget it all. You'll learn how to march and how to clean. You won't be allowed to leave for two years, and I won't be allowed to visit. There will be no math; there will be no lessons. It can be like this for any student. But as the son of a traitor, they will make it unbearable for you."

I stare at her. "Dad is not a traitor."

"Of course Dad isn't a traitor." She blinks the possibility away. "But that is what they will call him.

How else can the government justify what it has done—what it continues to do?"

"When were you going to tell me this? When I was already on my way to military school?"

Mom is unmoved. The truth seems to be giving her a new kind of strength. She hasn't finished.

"The sons and daughters of traitors don't serve two years. Some of them never leave."

"Never?" I gasp, searching her face for a clue that she might be making this up to scare me.

"After your training they'll send you to the gold mines. You'll work for sixteen hours a day but earn no money. You won't even earn the bus fare to come home—not that you would be allowed to use the bus, anyway."

I stand up. I have no intention of going anywhere, but I cannot sit still while my mother rearranges the pieces of my life around me.

"I've been waiting to tell you everything." Mom looks at me intently. "But I've waited too long. Saba and I had a plan to get you and Bini out of military service; we thought we had a couple of years before we needed to act, but you've both been pushed up through your grades so fast. We were proud but also frightened by the speed at which you were approaching grade twelve. Then when the soldiers came to our district, Saba decided to take Bini out of school. Lots of parents do it, hoping it will make their children harder to track. Out of sight, out of mind. But you are not out of sight or out of mind. The soldiers did see you, the evening when you went out to get injera. Now they want to track you down. They will be back. Maybe this week. It wouldn't take them long to find out that Bini is living next door, and he'll be rounded up, too. That is why you both have to go now."

"Go where?"

"You have to leave the country."

Her words don't make sense. "What about your business? What about school?"

"Shif, school is not important compared with your freedom. As for my business, that doesn't matter, either. The truth is that you'll be going without me and Lemlem."

I feel as if the world is spinning around me, breaking into fragments while I stand in the middle, watching, unable to stop it.

41

"I'm not leaving without you," I say.

My mother looks around the room as if the explanation I need is buzzing around it somewhere like a wasp.

"Shif, you must go. I don't yet have enough money saved for all of us to leave. You're the one in immediate danger, so you must go first. I've arranged everything. Some men will come for you and Bini tomorrow. Saba and I first got in touch with them two years ago. They're smugglers—their job is to get people out of the country. They'll take you to the border and then you'll be met by other contacts who can take you north to the coast, where you'll take a boat to Europe. Everything will be paid for before you go, but you must memorize my phone number and Uncle Batha's number in case you need more money in an emergency. There are other numbers you must try to memorize, too—of our friends in England. As soon as you've gone, I'll begin to save for me and Lemlem. We'll be fine. We'll join you in six months, maybe a little longer."

I want to say no. I want to point out a flaw in her logic, but I can't think of a single thing to say. There is nothing solid upon which to base my thoughts anymore.

I think about leaving Mom and Lemlem, going

so far away that we'll be separated by other countries, by seas, by mountains. We've never spent a single day apart. I feel my chest heaving and brush away tears before they run down my cheeks.

Mom stands up and pulls me toward her. She hugs me tightly, then pushes me gently away so she can see my face. "You must pack tonight," she says quietly. "A warm pullover, one change of clothes, some bread, water, and money. I'll sew the money into your shoes, just enough to buy some food."

"So Bini is coming with me? Has Saba told him yet?" I ask.

"She's talking to him tonight. You and Bini will leave together. You must look after each other. The journey will be much safer with two of you."

"What about Dad? He's alive. If I leave this country, I'll never see him again."

My mother doesn't answer at first. She places a warm hand against my cheek.

"If you don't leave, you won't see any of us again. I've told Lemlem that you've passed your exams early so you're starting your military training early, too. I don't want to frighten her. Pack now, then we'll eat together."

Lemlem bounces back into the room, clutching some bright threads.

In a daze, I open the wooden cupboard. The same wooden cupboard I open every morning and evening. I look at my four T-shirts and decide which ones to take. Suddenly four seems like luxury. I pack some underwear, a pullover, and my chess set. I take a plastic bottle from the yard and fill it with water. I stuff it all into my small fabric duffel bag and leave it at the foot of my bed.

"Can I go and see Bini?" I ask.

"No. Please stay inside now until tomorrow. We don't want to attract any attention. Anyway, Saba will want to spend this evening with Bini, and I want to spend it with you."

I want to walk out of my house, then come back and find that everything is the same as it was a week ago. I wonder whether Saba has told Bini yet. I wonder how I will know. Will there be shouting? Of course not. But will he just accept what she says, as I did, or will he refuse to go? It feels as if the course of my life, which had seemed so certain, is shifting like sand beneath my feet and might just suck me under.

We sit down to eat as if it's any other evening. My mouth feels dry, but I force myself to chew and swallow. There might be no hot meal tomorrow. Tomorrow I won't be sitting here with Mom and Lemlem.

I look over at my little sister happily shoveling stew-soaked injera into her mouth. I won't cry in front of her. She notices me staring.

"Can I come and visit when you're at military school?" Lemlem asks.

"Yes, of course," I say. "You're going to start school soon, Lemlem. What do you want to learn about?"

"I want to learn about horses," she says.

"Horses are very important. Make sure you learn everything there is to know about horses, then I'll ask you about them when you visit."

"Okay," she says shyly.

I try to keep my voice steady. "And look after Mom while I'm away."

# Snatch

I don't know what time it is or what woke me. It's dark, and I can hear Mom and Lemlem breathing steadily beside me.

I hear feet moving on the gravel outside, then a knock at the door. Silence. Then loud hammering at the door.

Lemlem cries out, and Mom picks her up and moves to the back of the room.

"Who is it?" she calls calmly, while motioning to me to keep quiet.

"Where's your son?" replies the voice.

"He's in the hospital," Mom answers.

"Which hospital?" the voice asks.

She pauses.

There's the sound of something heavy hitting the door, which moves in its frame. Lemlem screams. Another bang, and the door swings open, smashing against the wall. An oblong of moonlight fills the floor.

Two soldiers in pale-green uniforms enter, standing still for a heartbeat while their eyes adjust to the gloom. Their eyes fix on me and they cross the room in what seems like no more than two steps.

"Put on your shoes. Your military service starts tomorrow."

"But I'm only fourteen," I hear myself saying.

"Put on your shoes," repeats the soldier closer to me.

His eyes move to the bag at the bottom of my bed. He looks inside it: clothes, food, water.

"For school tomorrow," my mother says.

"He takes spare clothes to school? And a chess set? Were you planning on going somewhere?" the soldier asks me.

"No," I reply, realizing immediately that I should say nothing.

The soldier nearer the door takes out his phone and goes outside to make a call.

I put on my shoes.

Mom rocks Lemlem, who is whimpering.

Maybe one minute later, maybe ten minutes later, the second soldier comes back inside.

"Your friend next door has packed a bag, too," he says, then goes outside and talks on the phone some more.

"Say good-bye to your family," says the remaining soldier.

"I'll see you soon," I say, hugging Mom. I kneel down to hug my sister. "Remember to learn about horses for me, Lemlem." This time I cannot stop the tears from falling.

Outside is an old truck. In the back of the truck is Bini.

His mother is in the doorway to the house. I can see that she is crying, too. My mother stays in the house with Lemlem.

Without my bag, without anything, I climb up the

footboard and into the back of the truck. Apart from some metal bars the sides of the truck are open. The cold night air filters in, and as the truck revs and pulls away, I watch as my home slides past beneath the bars and disappears into the darkness behind.

I sit next to Bini, but right away the soldier yanks me up by the arm and pushes me over to the opposite side of the truck.

"Do you have anything—" Bini starts to speak.

"Shut up," the soldier says. "No talking."

I do not want to cry. I want to fold into myself, and keep folding until I disappear into a tiny dot that can drift in the wind back toward Mom and Lemlem. I can't see Bini's face properly in the shadow cast by the roof canopy. I cannot speak to him, either. But I am so grateful he is here.

There are two of us. We will look after each other.

# Journey

We sit in silence as the truck whines and rumbles through the center of the deserted city. The streetlamps cast pools of yellow light on the tarmac. As we reach the edge of town, the streetlamps become fewer and then disappear altogether. A new darkness descends, with smells of the dirt in the fields and of goats and sheep. The buildings are no longer square and smooth but scattered and round with straw roofs.

I desperately want to talk to Bini. Just to see if my voice still works. To see if I'm still me. Bini gets there first, of course.

"How was the test?" he asks quietly.

"No talking," one of the soldiers snaps.

Then I notice for the first time that Bini's lip is swollen and some dried blood is on his chin. He sees me looking and rubs at it gently with the top of his T-shirt.

After four or five hours, the horizon grows lighter. Later, the sun rises directly behind the truck, spreading a warm orange glow across our cold faces. We are heading west. My stomach begins to growl. My body doesn't seem to realize that the world is no longer the same.

As the sun climbs higher in the sky, it beats down on the canvas roof of the truck. Now I am grateful for the open sides, even though the dust makes my eyes sore and dries out my nose and mouth. I can see the landscape growing flatter. Yellow fields interrupt rocky hills, and the road has become nothing but bumps and dust.

"Is there water?" I ask. My first words, and my voice sounds whispery and hoarse.

The soldier looks slowly toward me, then away. "No water," he says.

My hunger begins to fade as my thirst intensifies. Soon all I can think about is bottles of water, of sipping cool water from a glass. I can imagine it vividly, which only makes the yearning worse. I do not ask again.

# Hell

We drive until dusk. I hear low voices near the front of the truck. The passenger door slams shut and we move slowly forward, then stop again.

The back of the truck opens, revealing three guards with rifles.

"Out!" shouts the one in the middle.

I jump from the back of the truck. My legs collapse beneath me—they have been bent for so long.

Bini jumps down beside me. "Stand up," he whispers.

The sun has nearly set, but I can see that we are

in some kind of compound. There are a few buildings. There is also some kind of thick fence or boundary that disappears into the dusky light. Beyond the boundary I see nothing but flat desert. I scramble quickly to my feet.

"Stay close," I whisper. I don't turn my head and neither does Bini, but I know that he's heard me.

I try not to shiver at the temperature drop. The buildings look like oblong metal boxes, each the size of a small house. The sides have a pattern of ridges. There are no windows and no obvious door. I wonder what they're for.

"Move. That way," the nearest guard says, pointing toward the second metal box.

Bini starts walking toward it and I follow, afraid to be more than a few feet away from my only connection with reality.

The guard bends down and shifts a huge bolt near the ground; the entire front of the metal box opens up as two doors swing back, and a terrible smell of sweat, dirty toilets, and something else wafts out from inside. I clamp my hand over my nose and mouth. Although it's too dark to see, I can sense there is something living inside the box. The guard pushes us toward the gaping entrance. Bini and I look at each other in horror.

We stumble over a step into the stinking darkness. The doors slam shut behind us, reverberating around the metal walls and ceiling and up through my feet.

I reach out and find Bini's arm.

"Don't move," he whispers. "Wait until your eyes adjust to the darkness."

I hear breathing. I can hear breathing all around me and the sliding of limbs. I focus on my own breath, in and out, my heart pounding in my chest.

"Who's there?" Bini asks after a couple of minutes.

"Shut up and sit down," replies a weak, rasping voice. "Don't waste energy." The owner of the voice sounds as if they are well practiced in not wasting energy.

"Stop using up the oxygen," says another voice, deeper and unfriendly.

There is an electric buzzing noise and a neon strip flickers above, filling the box with a sickly white light.

Suddenly the voices have bodies, too. Sitting around the edge are maybe fifteen men, with blankets draped around their shoulders. One corner is empty except for a bucket from which the rotten stench emanates, making my empty stomach roll.

We look around the room, searching for clues to explain where we are. Whatever Mom said about military school being bad, I know this is not military school.

"Where are we?" asks Bini.

"Your new home," says the man with the deeper voice. He is hunched on the floor but I can see that he is a big man; large hands pin the blanket to his knees. "I hope you like it," he adds. His eyes swivel up to look at us, and I can see a deep gash under his left eye.

"Stop it, Nebay," rasps an older man. The one who told us to sit down. His face is thin and grayish. His shoulders and knees seem to poke through his blanket, making him look as if he's made of wire, not bone. "Sit down," he repeats.

Bini walks to a small space between the foul-smelling bucket and the old man. I follow him and sit down.

"I'm Bini," he says quietly, looking at the older man.

"Yonas. And who's this?" asks the man, looking at me.

"This is my friend Shif."

Yonas nods slowly, reflecting on our names.

"So what did you and your friend do to end up here?" asks the old man.

"We did nothing," says Bini automatically.

You don't share personal information with strangers. Even if you are locked in a box with them.

"Everybody in here has done something," says Nebay. "Even though 'something' is normally nothing."

Bini looks at me.

I shake my head. I don't understand what he means, either.

On the opposite side of the room from the bucket, I see a plastic bowl and cup.

"Can we have some water?" I ask, surprised at how small and echoey my voice sounds in the metal box.

"So he can talk after all," says Nebay.

"Help yourself to water," says Yonas, "but don't have much. That has to last us until the morning."

I fill the cup but cannot stop at one sip. I pour some for Bini, then sit back down. As I look around the room, I see two men who could be eighteen or nineteen. The rest look older, the same age as Mom, apart from Yonas, who seems ancient. They are all staring at Bini and me with slow steady gazes. As if we are a television.

"No one new has joined us for almost a year," says Nebay, reading my thoughts. "We haven't had much in the way of entertainment since the radio broke."

A few of the other men roll their eyes and I understand that he is joking.

Despite the fetid air, the temperature inside the box is starting to drop, too. I want the guards to come back and take us to our real destination. I cannot believe they would leave us in this place for long. Perhaps they are trying to frighten us.

I know the men can hear every word that I say, so I choose them carefully.

"Bini," I whisper as quietly as I can, "what do you think this place is?"

"I don't know. But they asked what we'd done so it must be some kind of prison."

"Are you cold?" I whisper.

"Freezing," he answers. "We have to eat something."

My stomach rumbles painfully and I remember that I haven't eaten in almost twenty-four hours.

"Will there be food?" Bini asks Nebay.

"There will be two bread rolls each. It's the same every evening. That will be your food until tomorrow lunchtime, when it's soup. The guards will come soon. After that they will turn out the lights in here. Then it will be so dark you cannot even see your hand in front of your face, so have another look around and make sure you know where the bucket is. Whatever you do, don't piss on anyone in the night. You can share this blanket for now," he says, nodding to one of the younger men on the other side of the room, who peels the thin green blanket from around his shoulders and throws it halfheartedly toward Bini and me, then pulls a corner of the blanket on the man next to him over his knees.

"Thank you," says Bini. "We have nothing but the clothes we're wearing."

"We all keep our suitcases in the room next door," says Nebay sarcastically.

Yonas sighs, a loud raspy sigh.

Talking seems to exhaust them. Both Yonas and Nebay rest their heads on their knees.

"Is this a prison?" Bini asks.

"You should follow your friend's example and talk less," says Nebay.

After a minute or so, Yonas answers, "You're in a detention center for dangerous criminals."

"But we're not dangerous or criminals," says Bini.

"Do you think we're dangerous?" asks the old man, gesturing to the rest of the men in the box.

Bini and I look at the figures lining the walls.

They stare back at us.

Yonas turns to speak again, but before he can begin, there is a huge bang, followed by a creaking sound and the rush of cold air.

Three soldiers stand by the entrance. Behind them the sky is dark blue—it is almost night.

One soldier holds a basket of bread rolls, which he places on the floor near the door.

A second soldier tosses a blanket toward us, just missing the bucket. He peers inside.

"You." He points to me. "You are detainee eighty-seven. You are eighty-eight." He points to Bini. "Remember your numbers."

Then he steps back and, with the help of the other two guards, swings the doors shut again, sliding the bolt down with a clang.

After a few minutes, we hear another loud bang as the doors of the adjacent box are opened.

Bini throws the blanket straight over to the man who had lent us his. We still have to share, though.

A small man in the opposite corner gets slowly to his feet. He moves, it seems, as quickly as he can toward the basket, which isn't very fast. He limps around our cell, waiting in front of each prisoner as they take two rolls. His clothes hang as if empty, and his wrists and arms are as narrow as Lemlem's, just like the arms of every prisoner reaching up to take the bread. As Nebay takes his, I see that, despite his size, he is just as starved as the rest of them.

"Bini," I say in my lowest whisper, "will we look like this in a couple of weeks?"

"No," says Bini.

"Why not?" I whisper.

"There's plenty more of you left," he says.

I take my two pieces of bread. They are rock hard, which is good because it makes me eat them more slowly.

"Save some, if you can," says the old man.

Bini snaps off a chunk from one of the rolls and stuffs it carefully into his pocket, but I eat both of mine. The first one I barely chew before swallowing. The second I try to make last a little longer; my stomach can't believe it isn't the start of a bigger meal. My hunger feels worse, not better, but I start to warm up. I see most of the other men put a little piece of bread in a pocket or inside their shirt.

Then, as if someone has sent a silent message, they all begin rearranging blankets and making themselves as comfortable as possible on the metal floor.

Seconds later, the light goes out and we are plunged into absolute darkness.

At first I panic and feel my heart begin to race. I cannot tell if someone is coming toward me in the darkness, or whether the rustling noises are those of the men still trying to get comfortable.

I feel a cold hand on my shoulder.

"I'm still here," whispers Bini. "Let's wrap this blanket properly."

We move away from the wall and try to cover as much of ourselves as possible with the thin material.

"Remember when we used to get power cuts every evening at home? We could find the stack of candles without being able to see," says Bini. "That's the good thing about when it's really, really dark. You can pretend you're anywhere at all, so I'm going to pretend I'm at home in my house during a power cut. At least until morning."

"You think you can sleep?" I ask.

"We have to. Who knows what will happen tomorrow. We need to stay strong."

"Your friend talks sense," Yonas rasps. "Try to

rest. It will be freezing in here by the middle of the night," he adds. "Don't fall asleep against the wall or you might not wake up. Once the sun comes up, though, it will be a different story. The walls get so hot you could cook an egg on them, if you had one."

I stare into the darkness, listening to the men breathing and snoring. Every ten minutes or so someone starts coughing. I guess living in a box isn't very good for you.

Bini is completely silent. I desperately want to talk to him, but I know he's right—I should try to sleep.

I lie still, wondering if Mom can sleep tonight, and what she has told Lemlem. I wish I could talk to her, too. I think of the cozy room we slept in together, with its smells of cooking and soap. My bed with its comfortable dip, the same shape as my body. I never imagined that the first night I would spend away from home would be in prison.

# Hell 2

I must have dozed off eventually, because I wake as small circles of sunlight shine through the wall where it meets the ceiling, scattering discs of gold across the floor. It takes a minute to remember where I am. Then, with a wave of nausea, the previous day floods through my mind. I stare up at the circles again. Something so beautiful seems lost here. Then, slowly, I realize that the sunlight holes are bullet holes. Someone must have fired at the box to make air holes so we don't all suffocate.

My shoulder is numb from the hard floor, and my

nose and feet and fingers are numb from cold. I push myself up to sitting.

The two younger men are already awake, hunched against the wall. They nod at me.

Bini stirs, and a ripple of sniffing and coughing spreads through the box as men slowly emerge from their blanket cocoons like dirty moths. They look over toward me and Bini. Almost as if they are checking to be sure we weren't just part of their dream—or nightmare.

The last to wake is Yonas. He coughs violently for about five minutes.

Bini fetches him a cup of water.

"Did you sleep?" Yonas asks both of us eventually, but he's looking at Bini.

Bini nods.

The men seem able to talk to one another without us hearing what they say. All the same, Nebay shuffles over to Yonas so they can talk even more quietly. They mumble for a few minutes, which is all Yonas can manage without coughing. Even though I can't make out any words, I'm sure they're discussing me and Bini.

I try to talk like them—low and directly into Bini's

ear. "Do you think they'll come and let us out this morning? I'm not sure these guys like us very much."

"I think we're probably stuck here," whispers Bini. "Why would they spend a whole day driving us somewhere if they weren't planning on leaving us there for a while?"

I try to let his words sink in, but I don't believe them. "Do you think they've made a mistake? Maybe they confused us with some other prisoners and took them to military school instead of us."

"I don't know," says Bini. "Maybe they have made a massive mistake. Or maybe this is what happens when you try to leave the country."

"But we hadn't even gone anywhere." I realize that my voice has been getting steadily louder, and everyone's eyes are fixed on us.

"How long do you think they'll keep us here?" I whisper again.

"Looking at these guys, I don't think anyone gets to leave anytime soon."

A feeling washes over me. A feeling I don't recognize, caused by the thought that I have no control over what is happening to me. It makes my whole body seem heavy, as if I suddenly don't even have the energy to get up. My thoughts flick back to home, the smell of cooking, Lemlem giggling. I never sat still there, doing nothing. There was always school, homework, hanging out with Bini. An endless sequence of activity.

I feel a rush of panic as I think about the day stretching ahead of us. I cannot leave this room. There is barely space to walk from one side to the other. Bini is looking around restlessly. I don't know how much time has passed since we woke up. Maybe one hour, maybe two. I try to focus on something else.

"Where do you think we are?" I ask. "Which part of the country?"

"In the north somewhere," says Bini. "I guess we always wanted to see places outside the city. This isn't exactly what I had in mind, though."

He sounds just as he would if we were talking in my house—relaxed, making jokes. It confuses me. I want to ask him if he is scared like I am. If he wonders whether something worse is just around the corner.

All that comes out, though, is: "Do you think we're going to be okay?"

"I think we're going to be okay."

I feel a little bit calmer just hearing those words.

The other prisoners murmur rhythmically. A short conversation and then silence. Then more talking.

No one speaks to me and Bini, but I feel them watching us.

The box heats up as the sun rises. After several more hours, all Bini and I can do is lie dozing or staring at the ceiling, like everyone else.

There is a sudden bang on the door, which makes me jump.

"Time to let the animals out," says Nebay.

"Keep your head down and do exactly what they say," whispers Yonas. "You don't want to be sent to the punishment cell."

I cannot imagine anything worse than the cell we are in. But it seems someone has imagined it, and built it.

I will do exactly as I'm told.

The massive metal doors swing open with a deep creaking sound. I blink, shielding my eyes as bright morning light washes in.

Three guards in blue camouflage uniforms mark the doorway.

"Out!" shouts the nearest guard.

Bini and I are the first to step outside.

As the others clamber painfully to their feet, I see they all have limps or strangely twisted limbs. Limbs that look as if they have been broken and not healed properly. I feel sick as I picture my leg or arm being broken and then left to heal without any medicine or doctors to take away the pain. The sick feeling quickly begins to turn into panic as I realize that the guards surrounding us may be the same men who did these things to the others. I try to breathe more slowly.

Outside I see the camp properly for the first time. In addition to the four metal boxes, there are two small whitewashed buildings with tin roofs. Encircling the whole camp is a thick ring of thornbush. The sort used to contain cattle.

One guard pushes me in the back with the butt of his rifle and points ahead. He pushes me again, harder.

"Walk," Bini whispers, and starts to walk slowly in the direction the guard pointed.

"No talking!" shouts the guard. Even though I am right next to him.

We creep our way slowly around the perimeter. Beyond is flat rocky desert.

"Eyes down!" the guard shouts, and pushes me so hard that I fall to my knees on the stony ground.

I stumble quickly back onto my feet and we keep walking, the sun hot on our backs.

Barely ten minutes after stepping outside, the guard shouts, "Back to your cell!"

We shuffle away from the perimeter toward the second metal box in a row of four. Keeping my head down, I glance at the other boxes from the corner of my eye. They are so solid and so silent it's hard to believe people are inside them. I want to see who lives in the other cells. Maybe there are some other schoolkids like us.

The entrance to our cell gapes like the mouth of some silent monster. I step into the gloom and walk mechanically over to our blanket.

The other prisoners cough and wheeze, shuffling around to get comfortable on the hard floor. The short walk seems to have exhausted them all.

The box feels even more unbearable now that I have seen the sky and breathed fresh air again. I am waiting for something else bad to happen but don't want to start thinking about what it might be. I am also starting to feel angry. Angry that we have been put in here with no explanation and that someone else has decided all this without even talking to us. I move around, trying to find a way to stretch my legs without touching anyone else.

I watch the sunlight discs move slowly across the ceiling.

Bini kicks my foot.

"Do you have any bread?" he asks.

I realize how empty my stomach feels. "No, I finished mine last night."

He puts his hand in his pocket and takes out two small chunks of bread, giving one to me. I put it in my mouth. This time I don't swallow it straightaway but give my stomach time to think it's getting more than one tiny piece.

♟

I don't know how many hours have gone by, but I am starting to think I might pass out from the heat and lack of air, when there is another bang on the side of the box.

The bolt lifts and the doors swing open once more. A guard leaves a large pan of brown liquid and a stack of bowls on the floor. The smell of food and the rush of oxygen wake everyone.

As the doors slam shut, the small man who passed around the rolls gets to his feet and begins dipping bowls in the liquid and handing them out. It smells sour. There are lentils floating on top; otherwise it looks like muddy water. I have learned my lesson and sip at it slowly, even though I am desperate to pour it into my mouth in one gulp. It tastes like muddy water, too. There is almost no flavor, except a strange, sour, earthy taste. Bini and I watch the other men slowly sip the soup, making every mouthful last as long as possible.

The soup wakes up everybody. There is more conversation, but still no one talks to me and Bini.

Our bodies are exhausted from the journey and hunger. At some point that afternoon I fall asleep, waking only to eat my stale bread.

# Hell 3

The next morning, I stir as the rising sun glows through the bullet holes. I feel better, my body more rested.

Bini is already awake.

"That's the longest sleep I've ever had," he says.

"I guess it isn't every day you get sent to prison," I answer.

He smiles. "We made it through our first day of hell, and we are okay."

The others are stirring, rubbing their frozen hands and feet to get some blood to circulate.

Yonas coughs and looks over at us. There is something different about him today, a new kind of energy. "So are you ready to talk to us now?" Bini and I look at Yonas without answering. "What did you two do to end up here?"

"Leave them," says Nebay, his morning voice even deeper. "I don't think they have an ounce of courage between them."

Yonas is quiet for a while, then says, "You don't want to talk, of course. Soon you will realize that things in here are different from on the outside. Anything you were afraid of has already happened." He stops as more coughing takes over, making his body shake. Once it passes, he looks up again. "Do you know what this is?" He gestures to the four walls.

We shake our heads.

"What you are inside is, in fact, a shipping container. Some people may think of that as irony. Or perhaps bad luck," says Yonas. "These containers weren't built for humans—they were designed for anything that can be stacked up and sent somewhere on a ship. But then someone had a great idea. If they're so good at storing things, perhaps we can use them for prisoners. And instead of shipping them across the sea, let's ship them to the desert, where they can't do any harm. You can talk. Or you can keep quiet. But I believe it will be in both your interests to trust us. You don't have anyone else, for a start, and the days don't get any shorter."

Bini pushes himself up onto his elbows. "How do we know that you're not working for the military, too, and that you'll get special treatment the more we confess to you?"

"Bini, stop," I whisper. He is staring at Yonas through the gloom. "Maybe we can say what happened without telling them anything the soldiers don't already know."

After a few moments, Bini breaks the awkward silence. "There was a giffa in our part of the city. Soldiers were taking kids from the next street along. So our mothers arranged for us to leave. We had packed some things and were ready to go when the soldiers came to our houses. They found our bags. It was during the school week, and there were spare clothes and supplies in them, so I guess it must have seemed pretty obvious we were going somewhere to avoid the giffa."

It feels as if Bini has told them just enough, without saying that we were planning on leaving the country.

The old man clears his throat and begins to speak in a lower voice. "Before this," he says, pointing to the four walls, "I was a journalist. Do you know what that is?"

"Of course," says Bini. "You worked for *Haddas*?"

Yonas laughs, a short laugh that almost sounds like a cough. "When I was a journalist, you didn't have to write for *Haddas*—there were lots of newspapers; you could write what you wanted. That's what I did."

"It doesn't sound all that dangerous," says Bini. "Or, I mean, it doesn't sound like you were very dangerous."

"Well, things changed. Suddenly the government didn't want people writing about protests or about food shortages—about anything that made them look bad. So, as far as they were concerned, I was about as dangerous as you can get." Yonas laughs again, and this time it turns into a coughing fit that doesn't stop for a few minutes. "So they took me away from my three children and my wife and put me in jail. Not here, somewhere different to start with. That was fifteen years ago. I haven't seen or heard from my family in fifteen years. They haven't seen or heard from me. They probably think I'm dead."

As he says those last words, I feel the hairs on my arms stand up. "My father is in prison," I say before I can stop myself. "I only found out a couple of days ago. I thought he was dead."

Bini pinches my arm. "What?" he says. "Your father's alive?"

"Mom hasn't heard from him in six years. But he didn't die in the hospital, like she told me. She says he asked for higher wages for teachers and a man took him away and no one ever saw him again."

There are nods from the men around the room.

"You only just found out about what happened to him?" Nebay asks.

"Yes, four days ago." The words seem ridiculous. Four days ago may as well have been a different lifetime.

"Were you happy when you found out he was alive?"

His question throws me. "Of course I was happy," I say. Then, after a moment, I add, "I was angry with my mother for not telling me the truth."

Nebay is silent. I have shared more with people I've known for two days than I have with my best friend. They might bang on the side of the container and get the guard to come and take me away because my father is a "traitor." For some reason, though, I don't think they will do that. Maybe it's because they seem to understand what is happening to us.

I turn to Bini. Before I can speak he says, "Don't worry."

"About what?"

"That you didn't tell me about your dad."

"I would have told you. It's just—there wasn't enough—"

"I know." He cuts me off. "It's okay."

A short while later, Nebay's rough voice grates through the silence. "I ran away from the army," he says. "My two years of military service turned into four, then five. I met people who hadn't been allowed to go back home or anywhere for twenty years. So I ran away and they caught me."

It feels as if Bini and I are sitting at the entrance to a parallel world, where people are sent to prison for doing nothing wrong. Nebay's words are beginning to make sense: *Everybody in here has done something. Even though "something" is normally nothing.* We are all silent again, but now my mind has plenty of things to keep it busy.

♟

I don't know how long it is since we woke up. Maybe two hours, maybe four. I wonder how these men have lived like this for so long. Several hours feel like an eternity, trapped within four metal walls, which are quickly beginning to heat up as the desert sun rises in the sky.

There is a loud bang as a soldier slides up the bolts on the doors. They swing open, and this time I know what will happen. We shuffle toward the entrance and step, blinking, into the sun.

"No talking!" the guard shouts, even though this time we are all silent.

After a hundred yards or so, Yonas stumbles and falls. He looks too weak to get back up.

Bini rushes to his side and lifts him under his arms. "Lean on me," he says.

One of the guards pushes Bini away. Yonas wobbles but stays upright.

The guard has small mean eyes and thick eyebrows. He is a few inches shorter than Bini but pushes his face up as close to Bini's as possible and shouts, "Any more tricks like that and you will go straight to the punishment cell. What's your number?"

"Detainee eighty-eight," says Bini.

"Eighty-eight, do you understand?"

"Yes," says Bini.

The guard shoves Bini, who stumbles but manages to keep walking.

I keep my eyes forward. A warm light wind touches my face. The blue sky wraps around me, clear and cloudless.

Ten minutes later, we are back at the container. As the doors swing shut behind us, I want to run toward the last sliver of light. Instead, I wait for my eyes to adjust to the gloom and sit in the corner that now belongs to me and Bini.

Yonas lies on the floor, sweating. I fetch him some water and help him sit up and sip a little.

The container gradually becomes unbearably hot. Everyone moves away from the metal walls, and we all sip water to try to cool our burning mouths and bodies. Again, the others seem exhausted from the walk and the heat and lie in silence. I want to ask them when they let the men out of the other containers but decide my question can wait. Time is the one thing we seem to have a lot of.

Sweat beads on my forehead, and the darkness and thick air weigh down on me. I want to talk about life before the box. Normal life.

"Do you think our families are safe?" I whisper.

"It's us they wanted," Bini answers. "Now that they've taken us away they'll leave our families alone. Your mom and my mom will be busy working to save money so they can join us when we get out of here."

I want to believe him—after all, I don't remember any soldiers coming to our house after Dad was taken.

"You missed a couple of good lessons while you were skipping school," I say.

"Yeah, well, I reckon I can catch up."

"Do you still want to be a doctor?"

"Sure, why?"

"I'm not sure what I want to do anymore."

"What!" Bini whispers, pretending to be shocked.

"Maybe teaching would be good."

Bini looks thoughtful. "You'll have to get better at math, then."

I feel the start of a smile—and realize that my face isn't used to smiling anymore. It feels stiff and strange.

He is silent for a while, picking at the fluff on our blanket.

"Do you think my father really left home to find a better job? Why has he never contacted us? He could have been in touch just to let my mom know he was okay."

"Maybe he didn't want to until he could send you something."

"Maybe he didn't move to the other side of the city at all. Maybe he left the country."

I think about my mom hiding the truth to keep me safe. Hiding it so well that the lies became facts to me.

The guards bring us brown watery soup, just like yesterday. Just like every day from now on. I have already started to look forward to it.

"It makes a change from bread," says Bini. "Even if it does taste like watery dust."

Yonas seems better and manages to sit and eat like the rest of us.

After lunch, Yonas looks over at Nebay. Some silent communication seems to occur between them. Nebay nods; so does Yonas. I wonder what they are agreeing to. I wonder if Bini and I should be worried.

"Will we go outside again today?" Bini asks Yonas.

"That's it," he says. "They let us walk around the compound for a short while every day, like this morning, but otherwise we stay in here."

"The lucky ones also get to empty the slop bucket," says Nebay, "but the main event is collecting firewood. The guards are lazy and we're too weak to gather much wood. They'll choose you—that is, until you're in the same state as the rest of us. Every day you will get weaker."

It's true. Already I feel weaker than the day we arrived. Bini's face looks thinner, but I can't tell if that's just because he's tired.

"What about the men in the other containers? Are the containers all like this one?" I ask.

"You've seen that there are four like this, and there are some underground prisons, too, for punishment." Yonas pauses for a second. "The containers are all pretty much like this one. Metal boxes full of starving men."

"Why don't they let us all walk around the compound together?" asks Bini.

"There aren't many soldiers here. It saves money to keep numbers to a minimum. But that means they can't let all four containers out to walk at once—you can see how we might overpower them." Yonas snorts.

We are plunged into silence again as the heat saps the energy from our limbs and brains. Gradually, as the sun moves to the west, the heat becomes focused on the other side of the container. We crawl away from the sunny side.

I doze and wake with a start when the container shudders with another loud bang. The doors swing open and three guards stand at the entrance.

"Eighty-seven, eighty-eight, and forty-two, out here now!" shouts the guard nearest the door.

Bini and I get to our feet; so does one of the younger men. When he moves, he reminds me of my grandfather. Waiting outside are nine other men who must be from the other containers. They look curiously alike, as if staying too long in a box leaches away your distinctiveness. No one else is as young as Bini and me. I feel disappointed. I know it's stupid— we would never be allowed to talk to them anyway.

We shuffle behind the three guards, who lead the way to a metal gate buried within the thorn boundary. They unlock the padlock, and we file slowly past. It feels dangerous to be outside. I know I must keep my head down and gather wood, but the urge to run away across the desert is very strong. Perhaps they are testing us.

The guards lead us to a low rocky hill, where there are some thornbushes. We gather thin spiky sticks until the guards shout that it's time to return. We leave the wood in a small pile outside one of the white-washed huts. Two prisoners stay behind, straightening the jumbled thorns into even smaller piles.

Bini and I return to our container as dusk bathes the desert in orange light. I want to stay outside and watch. Instead, we climb back into the dark to wait for our bread rolls and another restless night in the icy box.

# Hell 4

The next morning begins like the one before. I wake early to the golden discs of light, only this time everyone else in the room is awake, too. I feel that something is happening. The hairs on my arms prickle.

I nudge Bini to wake up. He rubs his eyes, then looks around the room, sensing what I do. There are fifteen sets of eyes all focused on us.

"Did you get some good rest?" rasps Yonas.

"Not bad," replies Bini.

"Good," he says. "You will need clear heads today, and we don't have much time."

87

For the first time this week, I feel the urge to laugh but manage to stifle it into a snort. Locked in a metal box in the desert miles from anywhere, it feels as if we have all the time in the world but nothing to fill it with.

Although talking for long is hard for Yonas, he coughs, a signal that he may begin again. He takes a small piece of bread from his pocket and chews it slowly. My stomach twists painfully. I wish I had saved some bread last night. Yonas reaches into his pocket again and takes out a second cube of bread. This one he passes to me.

"Eat," he says. "It takes no time at all to end up looking like the rest of us. Come and sit here in front of me—it's easier to talk."

Bini and I shuffle around.

"How lucky we all felt when you two walked into our box." He smiles at me and Bini. A genuine smile of gratitude.

I feel the eyes of the other men on us.

"Our lives were over, but now we have a little sliver of hope," continues Yonas.

"I'm sorry," says Bini. "I don't understand."

"No, you've only been here for two days," Yonas says. "You couldn't understand." He coughs, then starts again. "No one knows we're here. No one even knows we're alive. We may still have our minds, but our bodies are wasting away. Even if one of us made it out of the camp, we wouldn't be able to walk more than a few hundred yards. We will die here, and no one will ever know the truth about what happened to us. No one except the guards, and we don't really count them as people." He looks straight at me. "Our families need to know what has happened to us. You understand why they need to know. We have a lot of time on our hands." Yonas gestures around the room. "A lot of time to plan, to think. But for almost a year now, we've understood that our only chance to take a little piece of ourselves to freedom would be if a new prisoner was assigned to our container."

I sense Bini sitting more upright.

"But that prisoner would need to be brave and would need to trust us with their lives."

Bini and I look at each other.

"Yesterday morning you helped me even though we were surrounded by guards. You showed us that you can be brave, but do you trust us?"

After a short pause, and before I can start to think of an answer, Bini says, "Not yet."

Yonas smiles. "I was right. You are brave."

"They don't trust us," says Nebay. "So what's the point? What if they share everything with the guards and we all end up in the punishment cell, one after the other?"

Somehow, Bini and I have become the untrustworthy ones. And we don't even know what they're talking about.

Yonas looks at us both. "Go around this room. Talk to everyone. Find out why we're all here. Then, when you've finished, you can decide whether we're worth trusting or not."

Bini says nothing more but lies back, his hands under his head, deep in thought.

It's my turn to pick at the fabric of the blanket as I try to ignore the tension in the box.

After what feels like a long time but probably isn't,

Bini slowly stands up and walks over to the man on the far side of the container who hands out the bread.

Relieved, I follow. We squeeze into a space on the floor in front of him.

"What's your name?" asks Bini.

One by one, we learn the names and stories of the men who share our prison. Some talk as if they are discussing another person's life, showing no emotion. Others have tears in their eyes when they describe leaving family behind.

We have nearly made our way around the whole container when we reach the two younger-looking prisoners.

"What is your name?" Bini asks the one who gave us his blanket on the first night.

He looks up but doesn't smile. Every movement seems to be an effort for him.

"My name is Hayat."

"How long have you been in prison?"

He looks as if he is about to answer but instead closes his eyes and shakes his head.

"I'm Idris," says the man sitting next to him. "Hayat

91

has only spoken to me about what happened to him. He won't talk to anyone else."

Idris looks at Hayat, and although I see no signal, it seems Hayat has consented to Idris's sharing his story.

"Hayat was fourteen when the military took him from his home during a giffa. He went to military school, where they beat him. After two years he tried to escape, but they caught him and brought him here. He hasn't seen his family since the evening when the soldiers came. He has a little brother and sister. They'll be twelve and fourteen now. He's worried about his sister, the older one. Worried that they'll take her, too."

I look over to Hayat, who is staring ahead. In the light from the bullet holes above, I see a tear snake silently down his cheek.

It seems that everyone in the container was captured trying to escape from military service, or trying to escape from the country. I wonder how many more centers there are like this. How many more people have been locked up.

Yonas is now the only one we haven't talked to.

We step over legs and blankets to where he is sitting, propped against the container wall. His head rests between two ridges, tilted up to the ceiling. His eyes are closed, his face peaceful. He could be relaxing in a cafe or his home. Only the paper-thin skin that clings to the bones of his face suggests that the image is incomplete. His eyes open and he looks across at us.

"You know my story." He smiles.

I feel disappointed. I want to know more about the man who has been a prisoner for fifteen years. How he has survived.

Yonas pauses, then adds, "But there is something more I can share." He turns to Bini and says, "I would like to speak to Shif alone."

Bini looks at me and I nod. He moves a few feet away to sit in our usual place, but he is watching us.

Yonas takes a deep slow breath in, then begins to speak in his special quiet voice, which, this time, is just for me to hear.

"The military came for me early in the morning. They took me away in a car, but we didn't leave the city. They drove me to a place near the president's palace where there were other journalists and people who had spoken out against the government. That's where this happened." He taps his twisted leg. "Afterward they took me to a different prison, with brick cells. The prison was large, but the cells were small and I was chained to the wall. I don't remember how I got there, but I know they kept me there for seven years. Next, I was moved to a detention center, where they used these instead of small cells." He points to the roof of the shipping container. "You roast and freeze, but at least there is company. Many people came and went while I was there. I remember most of them. There was nothing to do but talk and listen and sleep. After maybe three years, a young man came. I don't recall his name, but he had been a teacher."

I feel my chest tighten. I realize I have been holding my breath.

"Perhaps it wasn't your father. But there was something about him that reminds me of you. A calmness. He missed his family: a son and a baby daughter. His wife sewed for a living and he didn't know how she would make enough money to feed them. He struggled. But I could see that inside he was strong. He only stayed with us one month before they took him somewhere else. I don't know where. Our prison was packed to bursting, so chances are they took him somewhere bigger rather than to one of the punishment centers."

I blink away tears. I didn't tell Yonas what Mom does for a living, or that I have a sister. Lemlem would have been a baby when my father was taken. I calm my breath so I can speak.

"Thank you," I say. "That helps me believe my father might be alive."

Yonas is wheezing and has closed his eyes again.

I stand up and walk over to Bini. I sit down slowly and close my eyes to think. The heat is rising once more.

"What did he say?" Bini asks. "Are you okay?"

After a few seconds, I reply, "Yonas thinks he met my father in prison."

"You're kidding! Your dad was here?" says Bini, his mouth open.

"Not here. A different prison, a few years ago. I mean, maybe it wasn't my dad, but the man he met had been a teacher and had a son and daughter. His wife sewed for a living. He looked a bit like me."

"Then he must be alive!" says Bini.

"*Shhh*. If he was somewhere like this, and didn't do anything to upset the guards, then I guess my dad might still be alive."

"I'm sure he is," says Bini, sounding totally convinced. "Yonas is still around after fifteen years, and your dad has only been away for seven years. Plus he's younger than Yonas."

I wish I could call Mom. If only there were a way of letting her know that I'm okay and that it's possible Dad is alive.

"Do you trust Yonas?" Bini asks.

"I don't know if I trust him," I say, "but I think I like him."

"Okay. Then I think we should find out what they want," says Bini. "Anyhow, we're pretty low on options right now."

Light from one of the bullet holes highlights his smile.

I am impatient to hear what Nebay and Yonas

want to share with us, but the men are mostly dozing now. I begin to doze, too.

Maybe an hour later, I wake, under a blanket of stifling heat.

"So," says Yonas with some effort. "Have you decided what kind of people are sitting around this room?"

Bini sits up and rubs his eyes. "People like me and Shif," he says. "Or at least, you were like me and Shif when you first came."

Yonas looks up to the ceiling and mutters something under his breath. Then he smiles. He coughs a little, then says, "How happy we were when two of you walked in. Twice the chance of success."

"Success?" Bini asks, looking as confused as I feel. "In what?"

"We need someone to tell our families what has happened to us. After so long, it seems unfair that we now have so little time to prepare you. But you two are our only hope. Certainly my only hope—I don't expect to survive here for much longer. We're going to help you escape."

I feel a thrill of excitement, which quickly begins to fade. My thoughts are mirrored in Bini's face. I am wondering why no one else has managed to escape. It must be impossible to make it past both the guards and the boundary.

"What's in it for you?" Bini asks.

"Like I said, we need our families to know the truth. Then we can at least have some peace. But escaping is beyond us."

"Why didn't you try when you still could?" I ask quietly.

Before anyone has a chance to answer, Bini cuts in. "Is it because you knew you'd just get killed? I guess you've got nothing to lose if we go and get killed instead."

"That's a fair question," says Yonas. "Most of us came from other camps—we would have been physically unable to make it even when we first arrived. It didn't take long for those who were taken here first to end up looking like the rest of us. We didn't have a plan back then. By the time we did, it was too late for any of us."

"But they might decide to let you out one day," says Bini.

"I've been in prison for fifteen years, and in all that time I've never known them to set anyone free. Certainly the only way people leave this compound is with a sheet over their face."

"There's nothing they could offer us—that we want—apart from our freedom," says Nebay. "There aren't many perks here for good behavior. But if you prefer to rot with us, then go ahead."

"Escape and do what? Go back home?" Bini says.

"Keep your voice down," hisses Nebay.

"No," says Yonas. "Escape from this country. You will take the information you have learned about us to somewhere safe, and from there you will let our families know. You would be arrested immediately if you returned home. The military will be monitoring your houses, and those of your relatives."

"Our families," I gasp.

Yonas doesn't answer.

Once more I feel tears rush to my eyes, and suddenly I am very grateful for the darkness.

After a minute, Bini says, "I think I get why you want to help us escape, but we're stuck in this box, and outside there are guards everywhere. Wouldn't we be shot immediately?"

"Your opportunity will be when you gather firewood," says Nebay. "The guards don't get much more to eat than we do. They're unfit, and they're bad shots. You would have a chance."

"Has anyone tried to escape before?" Bini asks.

"Yes," says Yonas after a while. "They brought his body back the next day and showed us all what would happen if we tried to do the same."

I look over at Bini, but for once I cannot tell what he's thinking.

"What happens if we do make it away from the compound?" he asks. "Where would we go? You said we were in the desert miles from anywhere, so how can we ever leave the country?"

"Quieter," snarls Nebay.

"You're asking the right questions," answers Yonas. "We're miles from everything—except the border."

# Courage

The container gets hotter. I don't know if I can take much more.

Bini lies on his back staring at the ceiling, sweat glistening on his face.

I have no idea what time it is, but it feels like a couple of hours since today's brown soup. That means early afternoon.

No one has spoken for a while. Now that Yonas has mentioned escape, it's hard to think about anything else.

"Shouldn't we be making a plan?" I whisper.

"Finding out how they think we can escape? Yonas said we don't have much time."

"Look at them," Bini whispers back. "They're barely alive."

"Normally we sleep in the daytime." I tune in to Nebay's voice and realize he's talking to me. "But you're right; we need you to be ready in case you have a chance to go tonight."

I try to concentrate on what he's saying through the veil of heat.

"We're helping you because you're going to help us. To do that, you must learn each of our stories."

"We know them already," says Bini.

"Can you remember everyone's names? The names of our wives or parents?" Nebay asks. He doesn't wait for an answer. "You must learn the villages we came from, and, if there is one, a phone number. Test each other and, later, we will test you, too."

"Okay," says Bini, nodding.

"Also, there is one thing Yonas didn't tell you. The guards will interrogate you. It's standard practice. They will wait a few more days until you're starting to really miss your family and some decent food, until they think you'll tell them anything, and then they will take you away for questioning. Only, it won't be just questioning. By the time they've finished, neither of you will be running anywhere for some time. That is another reason why none of us was in any shape to escape, even when we had only been here a few weeks."

"But all we did was pack a bag," I say. "Our mothers had arranged for us to leave the country. All the guards know, though, is that we had packed a bag to go somewhere."

"They will want to know where to, who with, how. They won't rest until they have some answers."

♟

We are no more than halfway around the room when there is the now-familiar bang as the bolt slides down. The doors to the container swing open.

"You, eighty-seven, get up." A guard points to me. "And you, eighty-eight, and you, twenty-four." The guard points to Bini and the small man who served dinner. "Outside, now."

I step over to the entrance and turn to look at Nebay,

but the guard gives me a hard shove. Nine other men are already waiting outside. I'm not sure whether they are the same men as yesterday. We head back to the metal gate and the guards push us out of the compound.

"You have twenty minutes. Gather as much wood as you can carry."

Three armed guards follow us out and point toward the scrubby thornbushes at the base of the small rocky hillock.

I try to catch Bini's eye, but he is looking down.

We're not ready. If Bini runs, though, I must go, too. I cough to get his attention, but he is walking next to a guard and cannot turn around. I hope he doesn't think that's a sign for us to go. The sun is hot and my pulse is racing. Sweat sticks to my T-shirt.

The guards walk a little way ahead.

Bini bends down to pick up some thin sticks. He scratches one of them on the ground and I read the word *no*.

"What are you doing?" barks one of the guards. It's the one with the thick eyebrows and small violent eyes. He seems to dislike us more than he dislikes the other prisoners.

Bini doesn't answer but bends down to pick up more sticks.

The guard grabs Bini's collar and lifts his head. "You're not a student now," he hisses, scowling up at Bini. "Work faster." He shoves Bini to the ground.

Bini gathers the sticks he has dropped and carries on searching for more without looking up.

The guards assemble on one side, picking their teeth and talking. Watching us gather firewood seems like a nuisance for them.

When our arms are filled with thin thorny branches, we head slowly back toward the compound. The other men struggle to walk with their arms full, even though the wood doesn't weigh very much.

The guard with small eyes walks over beside me and Bini. "Tomorrow we will have a little chat with you, eighty-seven." He prods my side with his rifle. "You will need to have some answers. The day after, it will be your friend's turn." He smiles, but it is a smile to freeze blood, even in the desert.

There is silence as we step inside the container.

Bini and I sit back down with Semere, the man we were speaking to before the guards came. He smiles at us. Perhaps he is glad that we didn't try to leave. We pick up where we left off—finding out the name of his home village, a phone number for a close relative.

Finally, the only person left to speak to is Yonas again.

"Do you think you'll be able to remember everything you've learned?" he asks anxiously.

"No problem," says Bini. "It's much easier than binomial theorem."

Yonas looks at me, confused.

"Sure, Bini's right. It's pretty easy compared with what we have to remember at school." I pause but force myself to continue. "One of the guards said he wants to have a chat with me tomorrow."

I can just make out Yonas closing his eyes. "We will carry on as we are," he says. "The rest is up to fate."

My head swirls with names and stories of how the people in the room were first taken by the military. I feel as if the skin has been peeled off the country I knew, and now I see the rotten fruit inside.

"Let's test each other," says Bini.

We recite names and villages until the gaps between our answers become longer. Bini starts to doze.

I cannot stop from thinking about what will happen during my time with the guards tomorrow. I might tell them something by mistake that will put my mother in danger. Yonas made it sound as if they would hurt me. If I am badly hurt, then I won't be able to leave here with Bini.

The box finally begins to cool down and the men start shuffling around in their blankets, preparing to rest.

I turn to face Yonas and ask softly, "If we do make it out of the camp, then where do we go? How do we know which direction the border is?"

"For that," he answers, "you will need to talk to Tesfay." Yonas points to the bread man. "I know that he has a wife but no children, and he tried to escape from a military camp similar to this one, two years ago. Only, at that military camp he wasn't a prisoner—he was in charge of logistics."

As if the guards have been listening to every word, there is a clank and the doors swing open to reveal a figure with a rifle slung over his shoulder, holding a basket of stale bread. Bread must come first.

As Tesfay gets up to pass it around, Yonas takes

off his shoe and removes what looks like a sock from his foot. I look more closely and see that it is a small bag made from the same cloth as the blankets.

"I've been waiting a long time for a chance to use this. You can carry a small amount of bread in here," he says. "Saves time if you need to leave in a hurry, which you will."

On the far side of the container, Idris takes something plastic from under his blanket and holds it up. Bini steps over to take it, but Idris snatches it back.

"If they find this on you, then you'll go straight to the punishment cells and you might not come back." His voice is so much younger than his face.

I can just make out that he's holding a small water bottle squashed flat, with some sort of cord attached to the top.

"You tie it around your waist and then tuck it into your pants. The guards can't see it, and you'll be able to run with your hands free." Idris conceals it back beneath his blanket.

Before we can eat our rolls, Nebay beckons Bini over. He passes him a piece of bread two centimeters by two centimeters.

"For your bag," he says.

Bini looks at the bread, then at Nebay, and smiles. Before he can sit down, others in the room beckon him over and also give a small piece of bread, until Bini's hands are both full. Yonas passes me the bag from underneath his blanket and we carefully place each square of bread inside, murmuring our thanks to everyone in turn.

I'm not used to making new friends. Maybe they aren't friends, exactly, but I know more about the people in this container than any of my old neighbors.

As we are plunged into darkness once more, I am amazed at how quickly I have absorbed the shape of the box and where people sit. I understand why they always pick the same spot, and why, although it stinks, Yonas has to sit so close to the toilet.

Bini grabs hold of my shoulder and we step carefully between the legs and blankets to reach Tesfay.

"Don't sit on top of me," he says. "Stop there—you're close enough."

He sits very still, but I can hear his breath wheezing in and out. I know that soon Bini and I will sound the same as him.

"You want to know how to escape," Tesfay whispers, "and whether you might live." It's not a question. He wheezes for a couple of breaths. "With one of those I can help you," he says. "Assuming you make it away from the camp alive, you'll need to head due west. In the afternoon, your shadow should fall to your left, moving around behind you. At dusk, one of the first and brightest stars to rise will be in the southeast; leave it behind you to your left. After sunset, the moon will rise in the east; head away from it.

"If you run in the daytime, you'll probably die from heat exhaustion; if you don't, they'll catch up and shoot you. Late afternoon or dusk is best, but you won't have a choice. The border is approximately six miles from here. If you walk without stopping, it'll take you two hours to reach it. You have to get to the border before they send out extra troops to catch you. They won't expect you to know how to get there, which is in your favor. There aren't any roads in the desert, which is good. But they have trucks and they have guns. If you can run far enough to get out of their line of sight, then find some soft sand and bury yourself in it. They'll be looking for upright figures on the horizon. The border has a fence and checkpoints. The guards aren't always watching, and sometimes the towers are too far apart for them to see very clearly, but they also have guns." Tesfay continues in his special quiet voice until he seems satisfied that we know everything he has to share.

"And what are the chances of us actually making it away from the camp alive, really?" Bini asks.

Tesfay says nothing for a moment. "The chances of them ever setting you free from this camp are zero. Your chances of making it away from the camp are slightly higher than that."

Before Tesfay can say any more, there is a loud bang. I jump. Perhaps they have come for me a day early. Seconds later, I realize the guards are lifting the bolt on one of the containers next to us. There is a brief sound of shouting, then someone sobbing. Then the container doors slam shut and there is a hissing noise on the gravel. Someone's feet trailing in the stony sand as they are dragged away from the container.

We crawl back to our corner. I fall asleep with numbers, names, and villages running through my head, trying to block out the cries of the man who is being beaten in one of the whitewashed buildings.

# Fear

I wake as light shines through the bullet holes above me. A hundred small suns.

Then I become aware of the eyes upon Bini and me again. The other men are awake. Now, though, I see that they look at us with hope, not menace as I'd thought before.

"Time for me to test you," says Nebay.

We move closer to him, and he starts by pointing from prisoner to prisoner, choosing either me or Bini to tell him his name, what happened to him, and any details of his family we might know. Although we speak in no more than a whisper, I know that the men are listening to every word.

We get it all right.

"I thought everyone living in this box was going to die in this box. But now that you've arrived, that's not true anymore. Even if we don't get out of here, our stories might." Nebay says nothing more.

I never noticed it before, but my life used to move at a steady pace. For the last week, time has taken on a new dimension. I understand that it can accelerate in a heartbeat, then slow almost to a stop. I must learn to cope with a different rhythm.

The container gradually heats up with the morning sun.

"Want to play chess?" asks Bini.

I stare at him blankly.

"I'll go first. I move my king's pawn two spaces to e4."

I feel a smile creep across my face. I need to think for a minute. "Okay, I move my king's pawn to e4, too."

"You mean e5," says Bini.

"Ah, so you keep counting from your side. In that

case, e5." I find it much harder moving the pieces in my head.

After eight moves, it's checkmate. Bini beats me.

"Bad luck." He smiles.

"I hope not," I reply.

With every bang of a container bolt, I wonder if the guards are coming to take me away for questioning. But today follows the same pattern as the previous days; the container becomes hotter and hotter, until all thoughts are pushed from our minds and we begin to doze again.

I wake and notice that the temperature has dropped very slightly.

No one has come to get us. In fact, the camp is very quiet.

"Do they come at the same time every day?" I ask Yonas.

"Not every day, but if they do come, it's always before dusk."

The bullet-hole discs of light start to creep slowly across the floor toward the container wall as the sun sinks from its zenith.

A few minutes later, there is the crunch of feet in the

dust and a bang as the bolt of the next-door container slides open. They must be going to collect firewood.

Idris plunges the flattened bottle into the water bowl, holding it under for a few seconds, then screws on the lid, shakes off the drips, and throws it to Bini.

Yonas passes the bag of bread to me. I stuff it under my waistband, then pour a cup of water and gulp down half, then give the other half to Bini.

Bini is just rebuttoning his pants when the bolt slides on our container.

The guard peers in. "You, eighty-seven, and you, twenty-four, out now," he shouts, pointing to me and Tesfay. As he stares through the darkness, I feel as if my heart might have stopped. I can't go without Bini. He points toward our corner of the room again. "And you, eighty-eight."

We get quickly to our feet and walk to the entrance without turning around.

My heart starts thumping as if someone is banging the side of the container. I'm sure the guards can hear it.

"Act tired," whispers Bini.

As soon as we step down onto the sandy path, they slam and bolt the doors, then push us in the back with the butts of their rifles toward the men from the other containers, and then to the metal gate.

Once they have unhooked the padlock and we step outside the compound, I feel a thrill of excitement followed by a wave of fear. It is hard to tell them apart.

Bini and I shuffle like the others, perhaps even more slowly. I rub my eyes and stare at the ground just ahead of my feet, but my senses are drifting up toward the vast expanse of desert that surrounds us.

There is a patch of scrub where two of the prisoners start gathering small sticks. One guard stays with them while we walk closer to the foot of a low hill, where we were before. Thorny bushes and stumpy trees spread out in a semicircle around the base. I try to keep in step with Bini, but the guard pushes me along. We shuffle slowly toward one of the largest thornbushes and bend to start collecting some decent-size pieces of wood. I think one guard is still with the first two prisoners. The other two guards are with us. One of them hovers next to Bini. I carry on gathering sticks, my hands sweaty.

We must have been here for ten minutes or more. Soon they will round us up to head back to camp. I swivel my eyes up without lifting my head. One of the guards near us is picking his teeth with a stick. He raps Bini on the leg with the butt of his rifle.

"You should have twice as much. Faster," he growls.

He wanders over to the other guard—I guess to tell him it's time to head back. Without turning around, he unzips his pants and begins going to the bathroom.

Bini pinches my arm and I hear him muttering under his breath, "Three, two, one."

He sprints away from the bush toward the open desert. I throw my sticks to the ground and follow, zigzagging from side to side.

Seconds later, I hear a bullet ricochet from the tree trunk. Another whizzes past my head like a bee. Puffs of dirt jump in the air as more bullets hit the earth around us. We follow the curve of the hill until we are almost out of the line of sight. My thighs are burning and my mouth is dry. I hear shouting behind me but don't turn around. Bini is just in front of me, his arms pumping air and his feet kicking up dust with each pounding step.

The only word in my head is *run. Run.*

I try to imagine that the border is just ahead and I'm running to cross it. I reach the point where my legs are about to collapse and my chest is on fire. Bini must feel it, too, because he starts to slow. We skid to a halt and look over our shoulders. We can see nothing but the small hill separating us from the camp beyond. The sky glows golden with the setting sun. I hear the deep sound of a diesel engine revving.

We look around wildly for a soft patch of ground, running slowly with our eyes down. Bini points to a long crack in the earth. It's not very deep, but it's our only hope. We get down on our hands and knees to feel the earth on either side. It's not rock solid but isn't soft, either.

The engine is no longer revving but growling like a truck on the move. The noise grows louder, and it can only be a matter of minutes before we will be in the line of sight.

Bini starts scrabbling at the earth with his hands, like a dog, flinging dirt behind him. I do the same. My fingertips are numb and bloody after a few seconds. We don't dig down, but across, making the crack a little wider.

"Lie down," Bini gasps. "Put your head by my feet and throw some earth over your body."

We lie in a line along the crack, faces down, pushing our bodies as far into the earth as they will go. My chest heaves as I try to catch my breath. Sand and soil coat my tongue as I breathe with my mouth open, cheeks in the warm earth.

The rumble of the truck gets louder quickly. I feel my breathing stop as my body tenses. I pray that we look like nothing more than two rocky bumps in the uneven desert landscape.

The truck is so close now I can feel the vibrations as it whines and revs over the rocks and sand. I will myself to evaporate, to disappear, to become nothing but the dirt around me.

I hear shouting from the truck, and then the shouting becomes quieter as the vehicle speeds past us. The guards must be scanning the horizon for two running figures, unsure which direction to look in the gathering dusk.

I lie absolutely still. I feel Bini's feet at the top of my skull, motionless. Seconds tick past like miniature lifetimes. After maybe half an hour I hear the whine of a diesel truck coming back toward us. Although I haven't lifted my head or moved other than breathing,

I know it must now be dark outside. The truck rumbles past so close that some of the dirt kicked up by the wheels lands on my legs.

When silence returns, it feels deeper than before. No sounds of rustling blankets or coughing. For the first time in one week. Nothing.

Then I hear Bini move to sit up, dusting the dirt from his clothes. I sit up, too. We look in the direction of the camp and see nothing on the horizon. The camp itself is hidden beyond the small bluff, slightly darker than the sky around it.

Brushing the dirt from our faces, spitting it from our mouths, we look at each other and smile.

"I thought they were going to run us over," says Bini.

"That would have been pretty bad luck," I say. I feel almost dizzy with success.

"Give me some bread," he says, "and I might let you have a sip of water."

I chew the bread without sipping water. It sucks all the moisture from my mouth, but eventually I am able to swallow it. The water is so precious I save it for a small sip at the end of my feast of five cubes of bread.

"We can rest for a few minutes, then it's time to move," he says.

"Do you think we can make it to the border before morning?" I ask.

"Of course," he says. "We've been doing nothing for a week. It's time we got some exercise."

I smile again, then feel my smile suddenly fade.

"What?" Bini asks.

"I just realized, we've learned names and phone numbers for the other prisoners, but we haven't learned numbers for each other."

Bini tilts his head to one side. "For once you've had a good idea. I'll give you my mother's number and the number of my cousin in London. How about you?"

I teach Bini my mother's number, Uncle Batha's, and the number of our friend in England. We also recite the villages our relatives live in, although we already knew those.

"Just in case only one of us gets a chance to use a phone when we get across," I say.

He nods.

We start to walk. My legs are stiff; my stomach

rumbles, again fooled into thinking that the bread was the beginning of a proper meal.

After a few minutes, Bini breaks into a slow jog. We head toward where the sun set and keep looking up to see if the southeastern star is out. The air smells of earth, and the only sound is the regular crunch of our shoes in the dirt. We are surrounded by desert, with a dark blue sky fast becoming black overhead.

After a short while, we get into a running rhythm and my body starts to feel better. Still we are silent except for the regular thump of our feet. Then, without warning, Bini drops to the ground. I do the same.

"What is it?" I whisper.

"I think I see the border fence," he whispers back.

We must have been running for half an hour at the most.

"Isn't it too soon?" I say.

I'm sure we've only come a couple of miles.

Shuffling forward on our elbows like lizards, we stare intently but see nothing. The fence doesn't seem to get any closer.

"Bini, there's no fence. It's just the horizon."

"You're right," he replies. "It's way too soon. I guess I was just hoping."

"Do you think we're still heading in the right direction?"

Bini tips his head back and looks up to the vast sky above. The brightest star is still to our left, but now it has been joined by a silvery backdrop of smaller ones, so faint they give the impression of a universe that stretches away forever.

"I think we are, but we'll know for sure when the moon rises. We should get as far as we can before it does, though. We'll be much easier to spot in the moonlight."

"Do you think we'll be able to find some food once we've made it past the border?"

"Sure," Bini answers. "Don't you remember Tesfay describing the restaurant serving spaghetti and ice cream, just past one of the watchtowers? Maybe the guys in the watchtowers help with the orders, if they're not too busy."

"Ha, ha," I say, but the thought is so ridiculous that it seems almost possible. The fact that we have nothing but a small bag of stale bread and a squashed bottle of water feels less important than it did a few minutes ago.

"When we get to England, I'm going to eat ice cream every day."

"Will you still have time to watch Arsenal at the Emirates Stadium with me?"

"Yes!" I say.

Something about the vastness of the desert and sky that surround us has made us dizzy with excitement, even though we haven't made it over the border yet. It's as if we've reached an unspoken decision to savor every second before the next trial.

As we stand up, I become aware of a low rumble behind us and I see headlights shining in two moving pools. They are looking for us again, perhaps with more men.

The headlights are now facing in our direction. They're moving closer.

"Okay," says Bini. "Either way, we have to run."

But we're both on our feet before he finishes his sentence.

I run with my eyes down. The moon hasn't yet risen and the ground is uneven and covered in small stones. After a hundred yards or so, I turn to see the headlights pointing straight toward us, accompanied by the low throb of a diesel engine, as if whoever is driving the truck is no longer in a hurry.

Bini is twenty yards in front of me. I look up to see if there is any cover farther ahead. I can make out the dark humps of low hills to the left. I fix my eyes on them and focus on my pace. I must not slow down. My breath is rasping and I feel like collapsing to the ground but instead push myself faster. I'm catching Bini. I can hear the truck engine above the sound of my breath and the thud of my feet.

There is a puff of dust from the ground beside me. Bullets. Which means they are close enough to fire at us. Instinctively, I lower my head and try not to stumble. Bini does the same. There are more puffs in the ground on either side.

Bini shudders and yells out, then falls to his knees in front of me, clutching his arm.

I skid to a halt next to him.

"What happened?" I gasp, trying to catch my breath.

"They shot me in the arm," he pants.

I can see something dark seeping through his fingers, pressed near the top of his arm. Blood drips in the dust.

Bini stumbles to his feet and starts to walk. Each step seems to bump his wound.

His eyes are shut tight and he gasps, "Go."

The truck is almost upon us. Bullets whiz past our feet.

"Go!" he shouts. "Run!"

The headlights cast a bright-yellow glow around us as the truck bears down.

I look Bini in the face and see desperation in his eyes. I break into a run, my eyes still on Bini while he tugs the water bottle out with his good arm and throws it after me.

There is shouting from the truck and the puff of more bullets near my feet. I pick up speed. The truck is no longer following me.

I hear Bini shouting at the guards.

Without consciously slowing, I am aware of myself coming to a stop and then turning around to see Bini. He is swinging his good arm at them, punching and yelling. He is giving me a chance to get away.

I turn to keep running, trying to breathe through the sobs that are building within me, searching for the low hills on the near horizon while tears blur my eyes.

I hear two shots behind me, then silence.

I don't know how long I keep running until I reach the foot of the low rocky hills. I am aware of the truck circling around in the desert behind me, but unless their headlights shine directly at me they won't find me now. Bini bought me enough time to put at least five hundred yards between me and the truck. That is enough.

I scramble a short way up the hill. Dips and bumps offer some protection from the freezing night air. Thirty feet up, I stumble into a hollow between two rocks.

I scan the horizon one last time and see nothing but black desert, the areas of paler sand or rock highlighted by the rising moon. Somewhere out there in the blackness is my friend. I curl into a ball. My mind and body can no longer cope with being awake. I fall into a dreamless sleep.

# Border

Something crawls over my foot. I am half asleep. I open my eyes and try to look down without lifting my neck. I hear a small creature moving near my leg. If it's a snake, I must keep completely still.

A small pair of ears pokes above the side of my leg. It's a mouse. Perhaps it can smell the bread. I slap my hand on the ground and it darts away with a squeak. I am grateful to the mouse. I don't know how long I've been asleep, but hopefully no more than an hour or two. The moon is still low.

Although I no longer feel hungry, I eat two squares of bread and take two sips of water. It feels wrong to eat and drink.

Slowly, I stand up; the muscles in my legs and arms are stiff and aching.

I start to walk east. I am a robot, putting one foot in front of the other. The human Shif is hiding somewhere inside. I don't know if he will ever reappear.

♟

I walk and walk. I don't care about leaving footprints. The sun becomes a long thin glow on the horizon. I occupy myself by thinking about how long I ran for, and for how long I have walked. If my math is right, then I must have covered at least eighteen miles. Tesfay said the border was about six miles from the camp.

Either I am heading completely in the wrong direction, or his information about the border fence was wrong. Maybe there is a fence somewhere, but it doesn't reach here. There are no watchtowers, either. I must be so far from any towns or cities that the military decided no person could get this far without being caught. I guess it's easy to underestimate what desperate people are capable of. Perhaps I have passed silently from one country to another, and my only witnesses were the small creatures that live in the sand and rocks.

# Desert

I know that I must walk as far as I can before the sun is strong again, but somehow the reserves of energy I drew on before have completely disappeared. My body feels heavy.

I try to remember what Tesfay told us but find it hard to concentrate. I need something to focus on, to draw my thoughts away from the black hole that threatens to suck me in. He said to head southwest after the border. There is a refugee camp where I will be able to easily find someone who can arrange a journey north to the coast, and then on to a boat to

Europe. There are many smugglers, so I might get a good price. He didn't know how long it would take me to get there. Maybe two days walking, maybe five. If it's more than two, I am in trouble. Two-thirds of my water and half my bread are gone.

I am already weak after my time in the camp and so little food. I look to the south and see in the far distance what look like huge round-topped reddish mountains looming to the left.

I am glad that daylight has bleached away the dark, but there is still no sound other than the rhythmic crunch of my feet on the sandy gravel. I am tired in a way I don't remember ever feeling before. It's as if an extra layer shrouds my body, a layer of something heavy and persistent.

Wearily, I reach down for the bread bag at my waist and don't see the sharp stone directly beneath my foot. My ankle twists and I crumple to the ground. Pain shoots from the side of my foot to my lower leg. After a minute, my ankle starts to swell. I can't put any weight on it but I can limp, although this uses a lot more energy than just walking. I have no energy to panic.

The sun is so hot that sweat runs down the side of my face and dries before it reaches my neck. A layer of salty sweat coats my body, sticking to my T-shirt. I have almost finished my water. There is a small thornbush ahead and I decide to rest there until the sun loses some of its heat. I can feel what little strength I have evaporating.

Before I sit, I hear a low engine rumble coming from the direction in which I am heading. There is dust on the horizon and a truck is speeding toward me.

I throw myself to the ground, but it's too late—whoever is driving the truck has seen me. I sit still—there is no point lying in the dirt anymore.

As the truck draws near, I look up again and see that the men in the back aren't wearing army clothes but long dishdashas and bright keffiyeh around their heads. They are not soldiers.

A tiny spark of hope lights in my chest. Maybe they are from the refugee camp and have come to rescue me and take me there.

They are waving in a friendly way. They will

have water. I wave back and start limping very slowly toward the truck. My ankle is now so swollen that I can hardly bear to touch the ground with my left foot.

As I start walking, the men stop waving. The truck slows to a stop about twenty yards away. The men are talking loudly to one another and every now and again point at me. They are arguing. One of the men throws up his arms in the air and then sits down. The driver revs the engine, and the truck turns around in a big dusty loop and heads back in the direction it came from.

I sink to the ground again, feeling as if I am the last person alive in the world.

# Riddle

Why did the men seem pleased to see me but then drive away, leaving me alone in the desert? They could see that I am injured and have no bags with me. No food.

What if I haven't made it across the border after all? What if I've been wandering in the wrong direction and the men in the truck have gone to get a reward from the soldiers for finding me?

If Bini were with me, we could talk about what just happened, reassure each other that we'll still be okay.

I decide to eat three squares of bread. That leaves

me with four. I tip a few drops of water into my mouth, but there isn't enough left for me to have a proper mouthful. Then I sit next to the bush. I wonder whether, if I sit here long enough, my body will start to resemble the spiny dried-out twigs beside me. In a dry whisper I recite phone numbers and addresses to keep myself human.

When the sun is a little lower, I stagger painfully upright and start limping heavily in the direction the truck went. I will walk as far as I can toward the refugee camp. I will keep walking until I collapse.

# Help

The reddish rounded hills grow slowly closer and taller. They are unlike anything I've seen before—almost straight-sided and smooth, like the mounds of paprika the spice sellers make to attract customers. As I hobble toward the vast base of the mountain, I realize that what I see in the distance is not a camp, but a town. There are white buildings with green trees between them. In front of the town are fields of what look like palm trees.

My ankle throbs, but I suddenly feel energy

returning from somewhere. There might be water, food, shelter. But I will need money for water and food. Swirling in the heat of my brain is the memory of my mother sewing money into my shoes.

After two hours, I reach the first buildings at the edge of town. My head is spinning and I can't focus. My mouth is so dry that I cannot swallow. The sun beats down, but I don't feel myself sweating anymore. Some small boys and girls run past me, laughing and talking. The sandy desert gathers itself into a wide dusty road leading farther into the town. On either side are walled compounds and fruit trees; one of the fruit trees hangs over the street, creating a little shade. I need to look for the notes or coins hidden within my shoes.

I fall shakily to my hands and knees and start to crawl toward the shady spot. Stones scrape my skin. But I reach the cool sanctuary. The sounds around me become fainter, as if they're moving away.

Just as I am about to lose consciousness, I feel a hand on my shoulder. A man is shaking me. He says something in a language I don't understand and then drops a coin in the dust in front of me. It is gold around the edge and silver in the middle. As my head spins, it seems to shine with unnatural brightness. At home the coins are silver. They have the words *Liberty, Equality, and Justice* written around the edge. I don't understand the writing on this coin. So I did cross the border. This town is in a different country. My coins may be worthless, but no one will know me here. No one will be looking for me.

I look at the new coin and am grateful but know that I cannot get up to buy anything with it. It's then that I realize that if I let myself drift away again, I will not wake up. I think hazily about the people in the prison, about Bini. I am free and they are not. Somewhere people can help me.

I hear voices behind me. Two boys are walking into town with a donkey laden with onions.

I whisper, "Water," and point to my mouth.

One of them gives me a piece of bread.

I mimic drinking from a cup and they pass me a goatskin water bottle. I take a sip, then another. I wonder if they realize that they have saved my life. How many times can my life be saved before my luck runs out?

As the sun sinks lower in the sky, I decide to try to walk down the wide dusty road with my coin in search of a market. As the road curves around, I hear the beeping of horns and buzz of motorbikes. I can also smell food and cattle and gasoline. I find the smells almost overwhelming. My senses seem to have become sharper now that I am properly starving. I wonder how I appear to people passing by. Poor and homeless. Like the people my mother would give a few cents to, before the police came to shoo them on or take them away.

Around another corner I see the edge of a market. The stalls spill from a central covered square out into the street. There are sheets on the ground, covered with vegetables and baskets of spices, rows of banana bunches and mounds of grain.

Near me a man crouches on the ground; next to him is a basket full of bottles of water. I give him my coin and take some water. I put my hand out for change and he gives me some. I do not know how to say "hello" or "thank you" here.

Toward the covered central area I see a kiosk with a glass front. Inside are rolls of bread. I limp over slowly and give the woman my money. She is wearing a bright headscarf like all the women around me, not a white netela like at home. She gives me two rolls and no change.

I turn to find a quiet spot to sit and drink and eat. A feeling of loneliness creeps over me as I realize that although I am free, it's obvious that people are used to seeing boys like me because they don't pay me any attention; they look around me. I have a strange sensation that I'm starting to disappear.

What would Bini do now? He would find somewhere to spend the night. He would not give up. So I try to think logically. I cannot walk far because of my ankle, which has swollen to twice its normal size, and because I am very weak. Maybe I can find a quiet corner in the market and sleep there. There will be old food on the floor of the market. Some of it will be edible, I'm sure.

I've never been on my own before. I've never had to look after myself. There's always been somebody else to do it for me. It occurs to me that I might never see anyone from home again and an icy chill trickles through me. I would give anything right now to see my mother's face, or Lemlem's or Bini's. To ask them where they think I should sleep, where I should look for food. I want someone to take my hand and give me a bed, something hot to eat.

Perhaps I will starve to death here, on my own.

By dusk, the marketplace begins to empty. Market traders cover their stalls with big sheets of plastic, or wrap everything up in the sheet it was laid out on.

From my hidden place behind the sacks of flour and grain I see two men who seem to be patrolling the area. They walk down each aisle of the covered market, maybe looking for stragglers or anyone trying to steal the traders' produce. Three aisles are left until they reach mine.

There's no way I can outrun anyone right now. I scan around for somewhere to hide, but behind me are more sacks stacked on top of one another. I look up and see that beneath the low tin roof are metal rafters close together. If I can get up there, I will be safe from the guards. They are now only two aisles away, walking slowly around sacks and baskets that litter the path. They are deep in conversation. I climb slowly onto the next sack, using my arms and my good leg to push myself up. The guards stop talking and I freeze. They peer around the deserted market, looking straight at me. My body hugs the sack. After a few seconds, they resume talking and I haul myself up onto the next sack, from where I can reach the metal beams.

Rats scuttle nearby but I don't mind them. I curl across two beams next to where the wall meets the roof, panting. My arms feel shaky and my ankle throbs, but I have bread and water and shelter.

# Numb

I wake to the quiet chatter of market traders returning to uncover their stalls or lay out their wares in the street. My arms and knees are sore from pressing onto the metal beams as I slept.

I am cold. I lie as still as I can, listening to people going about their lives beneath me. From time to time I turn to speak to Bini, only to remember that he's not here. Like a shadow, I think I see him on a rafter next to me, or on the sacks beneath, but it's my mind playing tricks on me. Showing me what I expect to see. What I want to see. A flash of Bini's face steals into my thoughts without warning. He is shouting at me to go. Did he really mean go, or did he want me to wait with him while the truck drove toward us? Hot tears creep into the corners of my eyes. I blink them away. If I start crying now, I may never stop.

♟

I doze off, waking to the sound of the call to prayer. I lie still and listen.

Perhaps half an hour later, I realize how hungry I am. The last of the bread has gone, but I have a little water. Outside the covered market area, a man is lifting two sacks of red onions from a cart onto a blanket on the ground. A large colorful umbrella provides shade for a woman sitting next to the sacks. She begins to peel off the dirty outer layers of the onions, discarding them in a pile.

Slowly, I ease myself from the rafters onto the topmost sack and slide carefully down to the ground. I hobble toward the woman and point to the onions. At first she thinks I want to buy some, then she looks at me more closely and understands. She points to a spot on the ground next to her, and I get to work, peeling onions. It's methodical work, which gives my mind a rest. Once I have finished, she gives me a small coin. I buy two more rolls and head back toward the grain sacks and the rafters. People are too busy buying and selling to pay me any attention.

For what is left of the day, I lie there, neither asleep nor awake but drifting somewhere in between. The hum of the market is comforting. It fills any spaces in my head where thoughts of Bini could creep in.

As darkness begins to fall and the traders pack up, the stillness frightens me, but my body is so exhausted that sleep comes anyway. Rats run across my legs and along the aisles between the stalls below. Dogs bark and then are silent.

I wake properly when I hear the call to prayer. It makes me feel connected to the rest of the town. Everyone else will be waking now, too. I think about the men back in the container, waking to the discs of light on the ceiling. For a second I picture Bini in there with them, waking without me, but alive. But in my heart I know that Bini is not in the container, just like he is not here. I cannot let myself think about his body punctured by bullets. I try to remember sitting next to him in class—smiling Bini, alive Bini—but the image seeps away like smoke.

The market begins to fill once more. I watch the women shop; looking and testing, asking and then shaking their heads, ready to walk away until the trader offers a better price. I watch the traders arranging their goods; piling and shaping, weighing and measuring, shouting and laughing at one another. In the middle of the morning the market is buzzing with people. I cannot see the onion seller today.

I crawl backward along my rafter and slide painfully down the sacks to the ground, then hobble slowly over to the man selling pots and pans and kitchenware all made from shiny metal. His new delivery is covered in dust and his stall is busy. I offer to wipe down the new items and make them shine again. He nods and throws me a cloth. The coin he gives me will buy more water and bread. After that I will choose my moment to climb painfully back up to the roof sanctuary.

The next few days pass with little variation. My ankle is less sore, but I am getting slowly weaker, and I don't care as much as I should. I'm sure the traders know that I am sleeping in the rafters, but no one seems to mind. I realize that the Bini-shaped black hole is starting to win. Although I cannot bear the thought of traveling without him, I know that he won't be coming to join me. I also know that he wouldn't want me to live in the rafters with the rats. Nor would Mom. That's not why she saved every spare coin to help me leave the country. And if I don't take the information about the men in the container with me to England, then who will?

With no one to talk to I find it hard to make decisions. I also find it hard to truly feel anything is important. I know that I must not die in this town, that people are depending on me. But everyone I care about is so far away. I barely have the energy to climb up and down from the roof. I need a smile, a hug, a kind word that I can understand.

I lie for a while as these thoughts circle around and

around in my head. What would Bini do? He would make a plan. I must make contact with a smuggler, someone who can take me north across the Sahara, toward a boat. There is one problem to which I have no solution: I cannot speak the language here, and there is no one that I know or trust. Searching for an answer to this problem will stop the darkness from creeping up on me again tonight.

# Hope

A trickle of customers begins to flow through the market and I listen to the chatter, the words all foreign to me. A familiar numbness drifts over me. Suddenly several words float up to the roof, words I know. I turn around to lie facedown on the rafters so I can see who is directly below me. I catch my ankle and stifle a gasp.

A girl, maybe my age, is standing next to an older woman. They are both wearing colorful scarves over their hair, not the white netela of home. The woman asks for flour and I hear the girl ask if they can buy some sugar. The older woman says no and the girl looks upset. I never really talked to girls at my school. But now I want to shout something down at them. Say hello. Instead I watch as they walk away to another stand farther inside the market.

I feel a hollowness in my stomach that is not hunger. Although I must climb down to look for food, or offer to do jobs for the market traders, all I can think about now is whether I will see the mother and her daughter again. What are they doing here? They must have escaped like me. Was it easier for them? Are they looking for a way to head north, too? I move my left foot. I can bend my ankle a little without crying out in pain.

Seeing them, hearing them, is the hug, the smile, the kind word that I needed. Suddenly, it seems possible to do more than just survive.

The next day they come again, although not as close as before, and I cannot hear what they are saying.

The day after, they do not come at all. I picture them in a truck driving across the Sahara, smiling. I allow myself to wish that I had never gone out to buy injera that night back at home, to wish that I had never tried to leave the prison, to imagine that then I might still be with at least one of the four people I care most about in the world. Then I tell myself I have escaped from prison, trekked across the desert, survived on my own for more than a week.

That night I only sleep for a couple of hours, then climb quietly down from the rafters to the sacks of grain below. I look around. I see no one but feel watched. The security guards are probably sleeping. I have decided that today, if the girl and mother come, I will try to speak to them.

As the traders begin to arrive, I wait behind some boxes, hoping no one will move me along.

Soon after dawn, I see them, walking slowly through the stalls together. I stand up and then quickly sit down again. Beyond the woman and her daughter I see a man with a long scar on his cheek that snakes from his eye to the corner of his mouth. He is wearing a red keffiyeh, but I notice him because he is keeping very still. Now that I have experience in trying not to be seen, I can tell when someone else is doing the same. He is looking at the girl and mother. As they walk closer toward him, he turns his head away and then casually gets up and walks over to a woman with beautiful long black hair and a veil covering her nose and the lower half of her face.

I look back to where the girl and her mother were walking, but they have gone. I scan the aisles and then spot them walking toward one of the fruit sellers. I limp slowly along after them. I can feel my heart thumping as it did when I was about to run from the camp. I stop a few feet away. I cannot decide how to introduce myself, having had so little practice at meeting new people.

As the woman leans down to look at the grapefruits, she sees me staring.

"Kemay hadirkin," I say.

Her daughter turns her head sharply to look at me.

"My name is Shif," I say.

The woman says nothing for a few seconds, then becomes aware of the traders looking on with interest.

"Of course," she says. "Shif. I wasn't expecting to see you here. Where is your family today?"

I hesitate.

"I hope they are well. You must all come by later

this afternoon. Five o'clock. You remember—near the blue mosque."

I nod.

She points to some grapefruit, which the trader weighs for her, then she and her daughter walk away down the aisle.

I turn and limp as quickly as I can back toward the flour stall, feeling like a real person again. Why did she pretend to know me? There is a warm glow inside me. I don't even mind eating the spongy black bruises on an avocado I find on the ground behind one of the sacks.

The trader who sells chickpeas and other dried food is weighing out lentils, then pouring them into plastic bags, which need tying up. It is a painstaking and annoying job. I point and make a motion like tying the bags. He nods. When I have finished, he passes me a few coins. I buy a small bunch of bananas.

After that, the hours pass slowly as I wander aimlessly, trying not to attract attention, waiting for five o'clock. Just before four, I check the small clock on the counter of the bread stall and start walking in the direction the mother pointed to. I know it will take me a long time to get anywhere. Three blocks down, I see the crescent of a mosque rising above the houses. I sit on the ground beside a wall and wait, watching a small brown lizard zigzagging its way toward an ant.

Maybe ten minutes later, a man walks slowly past without stopping.

A few minutes afterward, he walks past again and says, "Follow me," in my own language.

I get to my feet and limp as quickly as I can behind him. He heads down a narrow dirty alley, then turns again to another alleyway with a green door at the end. He turns to be sure I am there. He looks beyond me, back down the alley, then knocks quietly three times and the door swings open.

As my eyes adjust to the dark, I see a small room with four people inside. They are all looking at me. The girl and her mother are there, and a youngish couple in the corner. The mother looks at the man and nods.

"Welcome, Shif," she says. "Come and sit down. You don't look as if you can stand for very long."

For some reason hot tears pool at the bottom of my eyes. I sniff and wipe them away with the back of my hand. I stumble inside and sit where the man points.

"Are you here on your own?" the woman asks.

"Yes."

"Did you come on your own?"

I stare at her. "What do you mean?"

"You have run away, am I right?"

I nod.

"Did you leave the country alone?"

I want to say that I didn't come on my own, but I am worried that all that will come out is a loud sob. I take two breaths.

"I came with a friend," I say eventually. "He is dead now." It's the first time I have said the words out loud.

"I'm sorry, Shif," she says, looking at me with genuine sorrow in her eyes. "We also lost friends on our journey here. I am Shewit." She holds out her hand. "Where is your family, Shif?"

"My mother and sister are at home. I don't know where my father is." I realize that not just the woman, but the young couple, too, are listening and nodding, as if they know exactly what has happened to me in the last few weeks. I cannot imagine anyone having been through the same things.

"Where are you going now?"

I pause before answering. Shewit is looking at me with interest. I feel I have nothing left to lose.

"I was supposed to walk south to the refugee camp," I say. "But I hurt my ankle and only just made it here. I couldn't go any farther. My ankle is healing now, though, so perhaps I will be able to leave in a couple of days. I want to go to Europe."

Shewit and her husband start talking in low voices. As they talk, I look around the room again. It is very neat. There is a pile of folded clothes in the corner. Through an open door at the back of the room I see a small courtyard, from which wafts the smell of a wood fire burning. They must be cooking dinner. It's been so long since I've eaten a hot meal.

My hunger must show because Shewit looks over and says, "Would you like to eat? We can talk more afterward."

"Yes," I reply.

"We have lentil stew and bread."

She gives me a small portion and I eat slowly,

feeling full after a couple of mouthfuls. She advises me not to eat any more until my stomach is used to food again. She knows of people who have died because they've eaten too much after nearly starving. Their stomachs have torn.

When we have all finished, the woman says, "You must not go to the refugee camp. A tribe in this area kidnaps people who have escaped from our country. They live in tents outside the big towns, but many can be found around the markets and bus stations, too, looking for people like us. They know that we have few friends and no relatives to help us."

"To send them back home again?" I ask.

"No, to sell them."

"To sell the people?"

"Yes, they sell them to be used as slaves. If they don't capture you on the way to the camp, they come and find you there. They have gangs who patrol the camps, waiting for anyone new. Children get good prices. But selling isn't all they do. They're experts. Before selling you, they try to get hold of your family's money."

"How? They don't know where my family lives."

"They make you give them a phone number for a rich relative or your parents—whoever is going to pay for your passage to the sea."

"You could just say no," I answer, confused.

She smiles, a sad smile. "If you make too much trouble, then they kill you, or sell you again."

"Like a sheep," I say in horror.

"Perhaps," she says. "Although the farmer respects his sheep. Rest now. Your body needs to recover from what it has been through before you can go anywhere."

# Friend

Wake up." Someone is gently shaking my shoulder.

I blink and sit up. "Where am I?"

Then I recognize the lady kneeling next to me. Shewit. Pale light creeps under the door and around the shutter.

"We're going to the market." She nods toward the girl.

I rub my fists in my eyes. "I'll come to help you carry things."

"No. It would be better for you to stay here. Rest your ankle."

I notice that the room will be empty except for me and the woman in the corner whose leg and arm are bandaged. She is sitting up but her eyes are closed.

"Okay, thank you," I say, but I would prefer to be useful.

Once they have left, I go around the room folding blankets and tidying the small space. In the corner is the pile of clothes, including some white netela, the type that women and girls wear around their shoulders and heads back at home. I wonder why they don't wear them here. I lay new wood on the fire and then go back inside to wait for people to return. I hear the distant sound of a donkey braying. The room is quiet.

Soon there is a soft knock on the door, and Shewit and her daughter walk in with several bags.

"It's our job to cook for those who are working or cannot cook for themselves—my husband and Genet and her husband," she says, removing her brightly colored headscarf. "You can help us prepare the food."

She points to the small courtyard and gives me a bowl of lentils so I can pick out the stones, then goes inside. I have watched my mother and Lemlem do it many times but have never done it myself.

The girl sits on the floor next to me with a pile of onions. We work silently.

After a few minutes, the girl puts down her onion and looks at me. "My name is Almaz," she says.

"Hello, Almaz," I reply quietly. I don't know what else to say, even though my head is almost bursting with questions. "Why aren't you wearing your netela?" I ask, realizing immediately that I sound rude.

She doesn't seem annoyed. "Because it's not safe."

"Why?" I ask.

"It's best not to attract attention. There are people looking for anyone from our country, and white netela are pretty easy to pick out in a crowd."

"I thought your mother said those people were mostly near the camps?"

"Not only near the camps. There are just more of them near the camps."

"How long have you been here?"

Almaz pushes back her headscarf. Beneath it her hair is braided in neat rows.

"Three months and four days," she answers without hesitation, staring straight at me.

"That's such a long time," I say, alarmed. "Do you want to stay here?"

Almaz laughs. "No, we don't want to stay. We want to travel to England, but my mother and father didn't have enough money to pay for the whole journey, so Dad is working collecting and sorting garbage. Back home he worked in a bank. They wanted to leave before I was old enough to start my military training, but we heard that the government was carrying out a giffa in our part of the city, and one week later we left. Dad had enough to get us here, but not enough to get us to the coast. Do you have money?"

I am so happy to be sitting next to someone who is dealing with the same things I am dealing with, worrying about the same problems. I don't even pause before answering Almaz.

"I'm in the same situation as you—my mother wasn't planning to send me anywhere soon, but they started rounding up kids in our neighborhood. She had saved enough money to get me to Europe, but not enough for her and my little sister, Lemlem, to come, too."

Almaz finishes peeling and starts chopping the onions. She is fast, and she can look at me to talk even when she is chopping.

"I want to leave as soon as I can," I say, "but I don't know how to make contact with a smuggler. I don't think I can wait for three months, though."

"Speak to my father when he comes home."

She has a way of making me feel that I don't need to hide things. Like she won't judge me. I wonder if this is what it would be like to have an older sister. I immediately think of Lemlem and feel guilty. I hope she hasn't been missing me as much as I miss her; her little smiles, her little games, the way she always runs straight toward me for a hug after school.

At dusk Almaz's father returns, and then Genet's husband. They seem tired, moving slowly as they go to wash their hands outside. I wait until Almaz's father has drunk some tea before asking Shewit if I can speak with him.

He beckons me over with an impatient wave of his hand. "I'm Mesfin," he says.

"I'm Shif," I answer.

"I know," he says. He doesn't smile but the way he looks at me makes me feel welcome. "How's your ankle healing?"

"It's a bit better. Maybe soon I'll be able to work a little."

"You could," he says. "Although it's better if people don't notice you're here at all. So you have no money?"

"I have no money to buy food. My family can send money for traveling, though."

He nods. "My wife has a kind heart. You're lucky she found you first."

"I'm very grateful," I say. "It's kind of you to let me stay here when you have little space to share. But I want to travel to Europe as soon as I can. Can you help me find someone who can take me north?"

"I can find you a smuggler. The trick is to find a smuggler who isn't going to cheat you, sell you, or kill you." Mesfin looks at me as if he is waiting for me to agree. "I've made contact with someone who says he can arrange for us to go." He gestures around the room. "It's safer to travel together. Who has the money for you?"

"My mother."

"Have you spoken to her since you left?"

"No."

"How do you know the military hasn't put her in prison?"

"I don't know." I realize that I sound stupid.

"I have no phone," Mesfin replies. He is quiet for a minute. "I'm going to see my contact tomorrow evening. I'll introduce you to him. He'll give you his phone to call for the money. We'll be leaving in two weeks, by truck. If you can afford it, I recommend you do the same. The chances of your arriving in one piece, or arriving at all, are much better if you don't have to walk across the desert. The truck will take you across the border to the port, then you'll have to wait for a boat."

I nod. "Thank you."

"If you can't get the money, you'll be on your own. We can't wait for you."

"What can I do in return?"

"You can help my wife and daughter. You can stay out of sight."

Almaz faces the other way as she sits outside preparing dinner, but I can tell that she has listened to every word.

When her father goes to sit with Shewit, Almaz turns and beckons me to come outside.

I crouch down next to her on the step.

"Will you travel with us?" she asks.

"I don't know. It depends on how much money I need to pay and how much my mother has saved."

"I hope you can come with us," she says. "I miss my friends. It's been just me, Mom, and Dad for the last three months, then Genet and her husband arrived."

"Do you have brothers or sisters?" I ask.

"I have an older brother but he went to military camp four years ago and I haven't seen him since. My mother couldn't bear to lose two children. Once we get settled somewhere, she'll send money to my cousin to try to bribe some officials and find out where my brother is and whether they can get him out. How about you?"

"Just my sister, Lemlem."

I want to let Almaz know that talking to her makes me feel like Shif again—not detainee eighty-seven or the boy no one knows. But I can't find the right words to say anything at all, so I look at my feet.

"I would love a little sister," she says.

"Maybe you can meet her one day," I reply.

That night, as I curl up on the floor, I think about speaking to my mother tomorrow. I will be able to tell her that someone may have seen Dad alive, and that he was okay, which means there's a chance he is still alive now. It makes me think about Yonas and the other men in the container. When will I have a chance to call their families? I doubt Mesfin's contact will let me work my way through a list of phone numbers. Maybe my first chance will be when I get to England. I go over the information I know about each of them until I start to feel tired.

Tonight there is no black hole waiting for me, just sleep.

# Wait

The next day I watch impatiently as everyone leaves for work or to shop for food. Almaz's father told me that my ankle must be completely better before I can risk the journey north, so I have to take it easy. I look around for something useful to do. Folding the blankets and clothes takes me five minutes.

The woman in the corner of the room, Genet, opens her eyes and looks at me. "You're busy. Why not rest while you have the chance?"

"I can't just sit still and wait," I say; then I realize

that sounds as if I think she is lazy. "What did you do to your arm and leg?"

"A land mine exploded when we were crossing the border," she says. "Two people we were crossing with were killed. I was hit with some pieces of shrapnel. We managed to get the pieces out, but the cuts were deep and I wasn't able to clean them properly so they became infected. Now that we're here I'm able to bathe them and dress them, but they aren't healed yet."

I feel shocked at what happened to Genet, but she seems very calm. "Did you know the people who were killed?" I ask.

"We had met the day before. The smugglers put some of us together in a truck that took us closer to the border. So they weren't my friends, but we had planned to travel together once we had crossed the border. It was a woman and her husband. They were both young, but at least they didn't have any kids."

Genet looks young, too, but the way she talks makes her seem more like Shewit's age.

"How long have you been here?" I ask.

"I met Shewit two weeks ago. She found us in the market, just like she found you. What about your foot?"

"I sprained my ankle running from some guards, but it's nearly better."

"You're lucky. I told my husband he must leave with Shewit and her family even if I can't go, but I know he won't leave me."

Although talking to strangers is becoming easier, there is a little piece of me that cannot shake the feeling that I am putting myself in danger every time I share my plans for the future.

A little while later, Almaz and Shewit return. Money is so tight that they cannot afford large amounts of anything; instead they shop every day for whatever is about to run out.

We will have scrambled egg sandwiches for lunch. I go outside to help Almaz prepare them.

"Did you talk to Genet?" she asks.

"She told me how she hurt her arm and leg, and that if they don't heal, she won't be able to go with you."

"I don't think I could bear to stay for much longer. The only place we ever go to is the market—the rest of the time we're stuck in here."

I think about playing chess with Bini, then push that away to remember how Lemlem and I used to fill our time at home; we normally played gebeta, her favorite game.

"Why don't we make a gebeta board?" I suggest.

"Yes! What can we use to make it, though? All we have are plastic bags from the market."

"Do you have any cardboard?" I ask.

Almaz disappears inside for a minute.

"How about this?" she says, holding up an empty tissue box.

"That would be perfect. Do you think you can break the eggs in half, so we can use the shells?"

She smiles. "Of course I can."

After lunch we nestle the half eggshells in rows in the tissue box, then take some chickpeas and play our first game of gebeta together. As dinnertime approaches, we are still playing. We stow our board on the folded clothes in the corner of the room and start chopping. It feels so good to be busy.

When Almaz's father returns in the evening, he eats in silence, then wipes his hands and beckons me over.

"We'll go to meet Ato Medhanie now. He's the man arranging our transport to Europe."

My heart flutters and I calm myself by running through the phone numbers that my mother taught me. Mesfin smooths down the front of his T-shirt. It occurs to me that he is nervous, too.

We step through the door into the cool dusk air, and for a second I allow myself to enjoy the feeling that I can walk out whenever I please. Even though I know it's not safe.

We walk along several twisting alleyways, then cross a wide, busy road. On the other side of town are some large compounds sheltering big houses within. We knock on the door to one of these compounds. A man opens a grate to look at us, then unlocks the gate, and we pass through into a large walled space. There is a big tree in the corner heavy with grapefruit. Pots and flowers are scattered all around.

In another corner is a table with two men drinking tea. We walk over. Mesfin greets them in their language and then pushes me forward. One of the men wears a white shirt. He has gray hair and a short beard and smells of aftershave. He greets me in my language. I can see that he is assessing me. I can tell he has done it many times before. He points to two empty chairs at the table, then sits back down. His friend wanders into the house.

"I'm Medhanie," says the man in the white shirt. "So you want to travel north?"

"Yes, as far as the coast, and then get a boat to Europe. To England."

He smiles a quick smile. "You have money?"

"My mother has saved money."

"Do you want to go on foot or by truck?"

"I want to go by truck."

"Okay. Call her and tell her that you need five thousand dollars. Then give her the numbers she needs to transfer the money." He leans to one side and reaches his hand into his pants pocket, pulling out a large flat phone. He types something in. "There's the country code. Now enter your mother's number."

My finger wavers slightly over the keys as I type. I cannot imagine how my mother could possibly have saved this much money.

After a pause, the phone rings. I am about to hear my mother's voice again—the voice I have longed to hear for three weeks.

But a man answers.

"Who is this?" he asks abruptly.

I don't recognize his voice. I look up at Medhanie in confusion.

He takes the phone and cancels the call.

"I'm sorry for you," he says. "It sounds like the military has your mother's phone. It would be better for her if you never call her number again."

I want to shout at Medhanie and tell him he's wrong, or snatch the phone back and type the number again. Instead I sit very still. Now I don't know when I will hear Mom's voice again. Perhaps I will have to wait until I get to England. There I will be able to call my uncle to find out what is happening. He will be able to tell me whether I can speak to Mom without putting her in danger. It feels like such a long time to wait.

"Do you have another number you can call?" Medhanie looks impatient.

I sift through all the names and numbers stored in my head, trying to stay calm and not to think about the military grabbing my mother's phone from her hand. I sense that this man will give me only one more chance. I choose Uncle Batha.

"Yes, I have another number."

Medhanie types in the country code and hands me back the phone. The phone rings four times, then a man answers. I do not recognize his voice, either, but I haven't seen my uncle for a couple of years.

"It's Shif," I say.

There is silence, then the man asks, "What do you need?"

"I called Mom and she wasn't there. I need some money."

There is another pause. "Your mother isn't at home. Lemlem is okay. How much do you need?"

"Five thousand dollars," I say.

There is another pause. "And what about Bini?"

"Bini didn't make it across the border."

"Will he meet you later?"

"Bini is—" My throat seems to seize up. "I don't think Bini will be able to meet me later."

"Call me back in one hour." He hangs up.

Medhanie is looking at me with renewed interest. "You came with a friend?"

"Yes, he was hurt near the border."

"So you're on your own?"

"He's not on his own," says Mesfin firmly. "He will travel with us."

"Maybe," says Medhanie. "Does your uncle have the money?"

"He asked me to call him back in one hour."

I sit with Mesfin while Medhanie talks to his friend, who has wandered back out. They talk loudly, laughing a lot, as if Mesfin and I aren't there.

♟

An hour passes quickly. Medhanie gives me his phone again.

"Hello?" my uncle says. "Your mother hasn't saved as much as you need, but I've spoken to Bini's family. They want you to have the money Saba has saved for him. With that you'll have enough."

"Please say thank you to Saba." But "thank you" sounds as if I am grateful for a cake she gave me. Not the money she had saved for her own son.

I read out the numbers for the bank transfer.

"Is Mom okay?" I ask.

"Your mother is okay," says Uncle Batha.

But before he can say more, Medhanie takes the phone from me.

"That's enough. It's not cheap to make international calls. When the money arrives in my account, then we can discuss dates." He nods and then he and his friend go inside, leaving me and Mesfin to let ourselves out of the gate and back onto the street, into the cold night air.

When we get back, Shewit and Almaz are laying down blankets to prepare the room for sleep.

Almaz comes over immediately, still clutching a folded blanket. She stares at me, trying to work out if it's good news. Perhaps I don't look as happy as she'd hoped. "Did you get the money? Are you coming with us?" she asks.

"My uncle has the money. If he manages to transfer it, then I'll be coming with you."

A smile spreads across Almaz's face.

I try to smile back.

"What's the matter?" she asks. "This is what you've been waiting for."

"I tried to call my mother but she didn't answer—a man did, someone I don't know."

Almaz's smile fades.

Shewit has been listening. "It was probably someone from the military. It's unlikely they'll do anything but watch your mother and sister," she says. "Your mother has been through this before, hasn't she? She knows what to do."

"My uncle said she wasn't at home."

"Maybe she's with your uncle. It's good for your mother and sister to be near family right now."

What Shewit says makes sense. I like the idea of my mother and Lemlem staying with my uncle. I hope Saba isn't alone, either. I'm sure my mother wouldn't leave her on her own.

Before Shewit finishes, Almaz disappears inside. She returns a second later, clutching the tissue box.

"Shif, I need your help," she says.

"What?" I ask, happy to think about something else.

"I need you to eat eggs for lunch tomorrow," says Almaz.

I look at her, confused.

She holds up the gebeta box—half the eggshells have broken.

"I dropped it," she confesses, "when I was tidying up."

She looks so concerned that I find myself smiling.

"Okay, eggs tomorrow. Perhaps we should buy extra—just in case someone drops a few."

She makes a face at me.

# Hunted

Almaz and I cook dinner every night. I never cooked with Mom. She and Lemlem were a team. But I never offered to help, either. There is no money for anything but lentils, flour, vegetables, and some spices. No one has asked me to contribute, so I make myself as useful as possible. I learn to slice onions and about which spices to add to the lentils. Almaz shows me how to soak garlic and ginger and is patient when I burn things because the pan is too hot or I forget to stir it. In the evenings we play gebeta. She beats me more than I beat her.

"Have you ever played chess?" I ask.

"No. What's that?"

"You have a square board, and different pieces are allowed to move in different ways across the board. You have to try to plan each move in your head before you make it."

"That sounds complicated," she says, but I can tell she's interested. "Perhaps when we get to England, you can teach me. Then I can beat you at that, too."

When she says this, she reminds me of Bini.

"What do you want to do when we get to England? What do you want to be?" she asks.

"I want to become a teacher. Perhaps math—that was my favorite subject. How about you?"

"I want to study paleontology."

"Paleont—What?"

Almaz laughs. "Someone who studies dinosaurs."

"Seriously? What kind of job can you do after learning about dinosaurs?"

"I don't know. Maybe in a museum, or something to do with archaeology."

"Where did you learn about it?"

"I can't remember. I think my science teacher

mentioned it once, and I didn't know what she meant, so I looked it up. I like history, but I'm not interested in the history of presidents and kings—I want to learn about the history of the world, from the very start." She carries on slicing chilies without looking up. "My mother wasn't allowed to go to school. She doesn't mind what I study, as long as I work hard. I like math, too," she adds, "but not matrices."

I nod. "Bini didn't like them, either."

"Who's Bini?"

"My best friend."

She stops chopping and looks up at me, but I cannot meet her gaze. "Is he the one who tried to cross the border with you?"

"Yes, that was Bini."

"We won't forget the friends we've left behind" is all she says.

I'm glad she doesn't ask me any more.

"How did you get across the border?" I ask. I'm not ready to talk about Bini, but I like talking to Almaz. "Did you walk?"

"We were hidden in the back of a truck—me and Mom and Dad. My father knew someone who worked for border security. He paid the man some money, and the man arranged for us to travel in the back of a truck, hidden under plastic sheets and sacks."

"Someone from border security helped you to get across the border?" I'm not sure whether to believe it.

"I know. It seems so stupid. And if you have enough money, you can get straight from the border to the coast."

Money never seemed to matter very much when I was at home, but now that I've left, it seems money can decide everything.

♟

Despite trying to keep myself busy, as soon as people leave in the morning the room begins to feel smaller and smaller. I haven't set foot outside for at least a week. I practice standing on my tiptoes, then dropping down onto my heels. My ankle feels completely better, and my ribs aren't quite so visible in my chest as they were when I first arrived. I start doing push-ups in the little courtyard. The longer I stay inside, the more I find myself thinking about my mom and Lemlem, and missing them.

Sometimes I allow my thoughts to stray toward Bini, but never for more than a few seconds. Just long enough to wonder if he was alive when they took him back to the camp, or whether he died before he even got there. Then I think about when Medhanie will get in touch with us again. Surely he must have the money by now. My thoughts seem to grow and fill the room.

But then when I look over at Genet, I realize that I am lucky. I am almost completely better, but her cuts refuse to heal and her fever has returned. Her wounds are starting to smell bad.

One morning when everyone leaves, I can't bear it any longer. Almaz and her mother are the last to go. Only Genet is in the room, asleep in the corner. I slip on my shoes, open the door as quietly as I can, and pull it gently shut behind me. I step outside and blink in the daylight, which hurts my eyes. The alley stinks but I don't care—it makes me feel good just to be somewhere else. I twist and turn down the narrow dusty roads until I reach the main road leading to the market.

Almaz is walking just behind her mother on the

near side of the market stalls. Despite Mesfin's warnings to stay out of sight, I wander inside and look up at the roof. I find it hard to believe that I managed to sleep in the rafters. It's Thursday morning and the market is quickly becoming busy.

I lose sight of Almaz and then see her again by the stall that sells lentils for a good price. Her mother is walking toward the fruit stall. As Almaz leans forward to pass her money to the stall keeper, I see a flash of movement as a man grabs the purse from Almaz's hand, then runs down the aisle toward the main road. He is wearing a red keffiyeh. She shouts and runs after him. Her mother sees what is happening but is separated from her daughter by sacks of flour and lentils.

The man dodges the other shoppers or pushes them aside. Almaz follows. She is nimbler than the man and is gaining on him. I realize that catching him could be a very bad idea. I jump over a sack of onions and chase after Almaz, swerving around women, who shout at me.

The thief crosses the main road; a man on a motorbike turns sharply to avoid him, and his bike clatters to the ground as he jumps aside. Then the man in the red keffiyeh does something strange: He tosses the purse toward the curb. I realize it's not the money he wants—it's Almaz.

Almaz reaches the main road and crosses toward the grid of narrow streets on the other side. My feet stumble as I look ahead to make sure I don't lose sight of her. She darts down a dusty street after the man. I skid to a stop at the top of the street. Halfway down I see that the man has stopped, too. He is holding Almaz by the waist. She has her back to him and is struggling to kick him or twist around to scratch at his face.

"Put her down!" I shout.

He doesn't even look up. He is much bigger than Almaz and starts to overpower her, dragging her down an alley to the left. She is out of sight but I hear her yelling.

I sprint toward them, ignoring the shooting pain that has restarted in my ankle. No one from the market is coming to help. I turn left and see Almaz and the man ten yards along the alleyway. When he sees me, he starts shouting. He has a long scar down his cheek.

I run the final stretch down the alley until I am beside them. The man is about six feet tall; I push at his shoulder and try to grab his arm. He pins Almaz against the wall with one hand, then hits me in the face with the other. I fall backward; my cheek and nose explode with a coldness that almost immediately turns to throbbing pain.

Almaz manages to dig her knee into his stomach. As he doubles over, I scramble to my feet and knee him in the head. He falls backward onto the cobblestones as another man appears at the far end of the alley and starts running toward us. I grab Almaz's hand and push her in front of me.

"Run!" I shout, but she is already running as fast as she can back toward the market.

As I sprint after her, I hear the crunch of gravel as the injured man gets up and, with his friend, starts to chase us. We reach the end of the street and cross the main road to the market, swerving around the motorcycle that is still lying there.

Shewit is standing by the edge of the stalls, looking frantically around. She sees us and lifts her hand. When we reach her, she pulls Almaz toward her, wrapping both arms around her shoulders. She releases Almaz only when she notices me, then grabs my face between her hands and kisses me on each cheek.

I wince as she brushes my nose. I can feel the area around my eyes beginning to swell.

"You saved my daughter. Thank you for saving Almaz." Then she turns back to Almaz and says, "What were you thinking, running after that man?"

Almaz looks down. She ran after him without hesitation. She has courage, but it seems to disappear with the realization that her mother could have lost another child, and of what that might do to her.

I scan the market but cannot see either of the men who attacked us. The growing crowd must have forced them to keep their distance. But the people gathering around us don't seem entirely friendly. There are some raised voices and a few people are pointing.

"Heads down, and walk," Shewit says quietly.

# Hiding

We pass through the doorway into the cool room, which no longer seems small and stuffy. It feels friendly and safe and hidden.

Almaz goes to make tea. While she is busy, Shewit soaks a cloth in water and passes it to me. I rest it gently against the side of my throbbing nose.

When Almaz returns, Shewit says softly, "A purse can be replaced. A daughter cannot." Then she looks at me. "Let me see your face."

I peel away the cool cloth. "Does it look bad?" I ask.

"Your nose might be broken," says Shewit, "but it's still straight, so you've been a little bit lucky."

When Mesfin comes home that evening, Shewit draws him toward the courtyard at the back of the room. I hear her talking quietly. After a few minutes, Mesfin returns looking agitated. He calls Almaz over and she sits down in front of him.

"Promise me you will never do anything so reckless again?" he says quietly.

"Yes, Dad, I promise. I'm sorry."

"You're very lucky that Shif was there."

Mesfin calls me over next. I crouch low, and he leans forward and takes me by the shoulders.

"Thank you," he says.

That night, although there are only lentils and chopped onion to eat for dinner, the room buzzes with conversation. It feels as if everyone has been waiting for something like this to happen, and now that it has, they are relieved, but also worried that the slave-buying tribe knows we are here—and that they want Almaz enough to try to grab her in broad daylight.

I think back to the truck that drove toward me as I stood by the thornbush.

"I think some men like that nearly picked me up when I was walking toward town from the desert."

"But they left you alone?" asks Mesfin.

"They turned the truck around when I stood up."

"Perhaps they saw that you were injured. Maybe they thought you weren't worth much in that state. A beautiful girl, on the other hand, is worth a lot of money," says Mesfin.

"Didn't anyone from the market come to help?" Mesfin asks Shewit.

"I think they were frightened, too," she says. "Or perhaps they don't like so many refugees passing through their town."

"In that case," says Mesfin, looking at Shewit and Almaz, "you two cannot leave this room again until it's time to go."

"Then how will we eat?" Shewit asks.

Mesfin turns to me. "You asked if you could do something to help. Now you can. You will go shopping for all of us."

I nod, feeling happy that finally I can do something useful.

I go outside to help Almaz with dinner.

"You look like a panda," she says.

I automatically lift my hand to my nose, then wish I hadn't as pain shoots across my forehead. "What do you mean?"

"Your eyes are black." She giggles.

"Well, I'm glad it's so funny," I answer, embarrassed by my appearance. "Next time I'll just let you get kidnapped," I add, but it's hard to stay grumpy when Almaz giggles.

After dinner, Mesfin beckons for me to come and sit with him.

"Ato Medhanie wants to see us tonight," he says. "We'll go now. It's safer while there are still people on the streets."

As I slip on my shoes, Almaz comes over and touches my arm. "Good luck," she says.

I follow Mesfin out into the alley, taking the same route across town as before. I recognize the compound by the enormous grapefruit tree in the corner.

As we knock on the gate, a coldness passes through me. If the money hasn't arrived from my uncle, then I will be staying here in this town on my own. I will need to get a job and cook and shop for myself while trying to save money at the same time. I will need to learn how to speak the language. It might take me a year, maybe five years, to have another chance to leave. Assuming I don't get kidnapped first.

But the thought that frightens me the most is being separated from Almaz and her family. They are the reason I am still alive right now. They give me the strength to keep going when Mom and Lemlem are so far away. I'm not sure I could start all over again on my own.

We walk through the gate and toward the table where the man in the white shirt is waiting. He is on his own this time but talking loudly on his phone. When he sees us, he waves us over to sit at the table.

"Coffee?" he asks, holding his phone away from his face for a second.

Mesfin nods.

Medhanie shouts something toward the house,

then continues his phone conversation, which seems to be making him angry. He cancels the call and slings his phone onto the table as a woman arrives with two small cups and a coffeepot. He looks at me. "What happened to your face?"

"Nothing. Just a fight," I answer.

Medhanie nods, as if he isn't surprised. "Your uncle must care about you. The money has arrived." He looks at Mesfin. "You'll pay me the rest of what you owe tomorrow?"

Mesfin nods. "As soon as I've finished work."

"Good. Then it's time to tell you what will happen next. Before I do, any questions?"

I can't think of anything to ask. I know Bini would have thought of something important. So would Almaz.

He explains details of the pickup and the journey, then shakes our hands.

"I'll be waiting by the truck on Monday to oversee the operation," he says.

When we get home, Shewit and Almaz come silently over to greet us. Shewit points to Genet and her husband asleep on the floor, so we gather outside in the small courtyard, crouching among the pots and pans.

"Shif is coming with us," says Mesfin.

Shewit reaches over and hugs me; then Almaz does, too. I feel included, part of something good.

"On Monday evening some men will come to the house and take us to the truck," Mesfin explains. "We'll be provided with water and food, but we must wear as many clothes as we can because there won't be space for luggage—maybe one bag between us. Medhanie said the truck is a new one and we might reach the border to the north of the desert in five days. We'll be met there by some of his contacts, who will drive the final stretch to the port. We must wait there until the boat is ready to take us, then we sail for Italy."

That night I lie in bed staring at the ceiling. There are only three days between now and the truck to freedom.

Almaz is lying next to her mother on the other side of the room. Moonlight glows around the edge of the shutters and I see that her eyes are open, too.

I run through the list of names and phone numbers to try to calm myself. Mom taught me the number for her friend who lives in England. Once I arrive there, I am to call her first, and then call Mom to let her know that I'm okay. Only now I won't be able to call Mom.

I wonder what school is like in England. I will never make another friend like Bini, but will I make any friends at all? I can speak pretty good English, but our teacher had never met a native English speaker and guessed at how words should actually sound. Perhaps no one in England will be able to understand me.

♟

I wake early as usual, feeling groggy from little sleep.

The others are stretching and yawning. Genet is the only one lying still. Her husband takes a small cup of tea over to her and sits down quietly, stroking her hair. Genet's leg has started to turn a bluish color. There is no money for a doctor. Everything her husband earns goes toward the fee for Medhanie.

Almaz goes outside to boil water but her father calls her back. Normally Mesfin is at work by now. He beckons for me to come and sit by him, Shewit, and Almaz.

"The men at work say that someone has been asking questions about me. I think the kidnappers are angry that Almaz escaped from them and they want to find us. All of us. Even if not to sell, then to punish. Take this money." He hands me a small bundle of dirty notes. He looks at Shewit. "There isn't much. I won't be able to work today, and I needed to take out some extra money to make up the final payment for Ato Medhanie. Tell Shif what he needs to buy with it. This is the last time anyone will go to the market, so we must have food for the next few days, even if it's just lentils." He looks at me again. "Be quick, and make sure no one follows you. I'm going to take the money to Ato Medhanie now."

As I slip on my shoes, Almaz passes me the shopping bags.

"Be careful," she says.

I nod and silently leave the house.

As soon as I arrive at the market, I can tell that something is different. I walk toward the trader I've seen Almaz visit before to buy lentils for a good price. Around me is the normal hum of conversation, punctuated by a motorcycle horn or a shout, but the trader doesn't chat in the relaxed way he usually does. He barely looks up as he gathers my order.

I notice a short man standing in the shadows near where I spent my first few nights in the market. He is watching me but turns away when he sees me looking. I scan the market and notice another man standing at the far edge of the traders, next to the road. He doesn't look as if he's buying anything; he's just leaning against one of the poles, picking his teeth with a stick. He is wearing a blue keffiyeh, but I recognize him. It's the man with the scar.

I pay for the food, gathering my bags together in one hand, and walk away from the stall, careful not to look as if I am hurrying. As I reach the edge of the market, both men peel away from their resting places and begin to walk slowly in the same direction as me.

I cross the road next to the market, but instead of following the network of streets home, I turn the corner onto the busy main road that runs through the center of town. I start to run, zigzagging around shoppers and coffee sellers.

After fifty yards I turn to see that the two men are still following me, looking left and right at the junction of the main road. Ahead is the movie theater. I step off the sidewalk toward the wide entrance doors. The main doors are padlocked, but around the side a door is ajar. I run over and push my way inside, kicking a bucket and mop to one side. I click the door shut and crouch down in the dark, waiting for my breathing to slow.

The handle of the door turns and a lady wearing a pink headscarf peers around the door. She lets out a squeal of surprise when she sees me.

"Sorry," I say, lowering the shopping bags and raising my empty hands in the air, but the lady still looks fearful, unsure what to do next.

I grab a big white floorcloth from the shelf of supplies and the bags of shopping before squeezing past her, back out into the blinding morning light. I wrap the thin cloth around my head and then, looking down, carry on walking along the main road. I will find a different route home that doesn't go past the market.

I want to know if I'm being followed but do not turn around. After fifty feet I bear right off the main road.

Away from the traffic, it seems quiet. The street

is empty. I listen for the crunch of footsteps behind me. I turn right, and then right again, hoping that my sense of direction will lead me closer to home. Soon I recognize the narrow street leading up to our alley.

I reach the front door and knock softly in the rhythm we have agreed on. As I step out of the sun and into the cool dark, I notice that my back is damp with sweat.

"There were two men waiting for me at the market," I say to the room of faces all focused on me.

Mesfin has already returned from delivering the money. He locks the door and then goes over to the window, peering out through a gap behind the shutters. "Did they follow you?"

"No, I lost them at the movie theater."

Almaz giggles, and I realize that I am smiling, too. Perhaps because I am still free. Perhaps because losing your kidnappers at the movie theater sounds ridiculous.

♟

It's obvious we will be unable to leave the compound again until Monday, when we will leave forever.

We open the few bags of food we have. There is perhaps just enough to last until then, but nothing extra to take for the journey. Shewit tends to Genet, so Almaz and I begin our normal lunchtime routine of chopping and stirring. She is fast and methodical. I am messy, even though I try to follow her example. I find that cooking with Almaz makes me feel calm.

"You're getting pretty good," she says. "Maybe you should train as a chef in England instead of teaching."

I laugh. "I like cooking, but my favorite part is eating."

After a moment or two of silence, I ask, "Did you know that we'll be sailing to Italy instead of England?"

"Not until you came back that night with Dad and told us. But Dad says we don't have any good contacts in Italy, and it's harder to find work. We'll have to find a way to get to England from Italy."

"I'd love to eat a real Italian pizza," I say. "But all of my contacts are in England, too, and now that I can't call my mom, I have to make sure I'm easy for her to find. Did your friends know you were going to leave?"

"No. No one knew. Dad said we couldn't say anything, and that the most important thing was to carry on like normal. On my last day at school, I knew I wasn't going to see any of my friends again, but I couldn't even say good-bye. I had to pretend I would see them all the next morning."

Almaz pours a little water into the pan. It sizzles and a jet of burnt-onion steam billows out. She doesn't normally burn things.

The next few days pass slowly. We try to keep ourselves busy by choosing what to pack and what to leave, which takes very little time as we don't have much among us. Shewit mends the zipper on her big laundry bag, which we're going to squash everything into.

I exercise my ankle, which started to bother me again after running twice from the kidnappers.

Almaz spends time with a needle and thread, stitching a neat pattern around the bottom edge of her netela. It reminds me of evenings at home, when Mom brought back work to finish.

We play a lot of gebeta, even though four of the

eggshell cups are broken and we are unable to replace them.

On Sunday night, we get ready to sleep in the same room for the last time.

In the morning, Shewit goes to sit with Genet and her husband. They speak quietly for some time. Genet starts crying and Shewit hugs her.

Genet's fever is worse, and she seems weaker every day. I know that Shewit thinks Genet should go to the hospital and see what they can do for her. Otherwise her leg will turn septic and she will die. Her husband is worried about leaving her in the hospital alone, and about how he will pay for the treatment. There is no way they can travel with us.

When they have finished talking, Almaz goes over to Genet and gives her one of her two brightly colored headscarves.

When Almaz gets up, it is my turn.

I say good-bye to Genet's husband. He will have to work, shop, and cook for both of them now.

Then I turn to speak to Genet. "I hope that you can follow us in a couple of months when your leg is better."

She looks up at me and smiles a weak smile. Sometimes it's easier to smile than to speak when you are feeling broken.

♟

Shortly after lunch there is a knock at the door.

"Who is it?" Mesfin asks.

"It's time to leave," replies an impatient voice in English.

Shewit and Almaz kiss Genet on the cheeks. She smiles, but the smile quickly fades.

I pick up the large striped laundry bag; Almaz grabs on to one of my arms as the four of us step outside.

Two men with rifles are waiting in the alleyway. "Try not to walk in a line behind us. Keep your heads down. Let's go."

I am leaving another home, but this time the destination is Europe. I try not to let excitement take over. When I left prison, Tesfay said the chances of making it were barely higher than zero. The odds for this journey must be higher. A wave of sadness rushes over me. I was supposed to look after Bini. We were supposed to look after each other. He made sure I escaped; I left him to die.

Maybe Almaz and her family are foolish to let me travel with them.

We follow silently through the maze of streets until we reach the main road. We are less conspicuous here among the dust lifted by the cars and trucks, and the people hurrying along beside the traffic. The armed men walk fast, and I find it hard to keep up. The laundry bag is an awkward shape. I have to carry it in front of me and I can barely see where I'm going. I feel sweat running down my back.

We reach the edge of town, where there is a patch of dirt the size of two soccer fields; it is noisy with buses, coaches, and taxis.

Almaz is walking next to her mother; both have their eyes to the ground.

I walk with Mesfin. Since I rescued Almaz, he has started treating me more like a member of the family. We even played gebeta together a few times. I wonder how he feels, taking his wife and daughter from their safe room to journey across the desert. I guess their room wasn't going to be safe for much longer.

At the far edge of the bus depot is a large open-top truck with sixty or seventy people crammed inside. Yellow plastic containers drape over the sides, making it bulge like a pregnant donkey. I instantly know that this is the truck we will be traveling on. The little I can see of the actual truck is battered and dusty, and there is no shelter from the sun for the passengers. It is definitely not new, like Medhanie promised us. I cannot see him anywhere. Perhaps he is busy today after all.

One of the armed men takes a crumpled piece of paper from his pocket. "Name?" He looks at me.

"Shiferwa Gebreselassie."

He stops in front of Almaz and smiles at her, but it is not a friendly smile. "Name?"

I can barely hear her reply as she speaks to the ground, not wishing to meet the man's eyes.

The other man with a rifle is tall and has a curved nose that looks as if it may have been broken. He addresses all four of us. "The yellow containers are for fuel and water. Do not help yourselves. We'll stop to eat and drink, and you'll be given water then. If the road is good, it should take perhaps five or six days to cross the desert. You will be met at the border, where you'll take a different truck to the port. Understand?"

We all nod mutely.

"Find a space on top. If there's no room for your bag, you have to leave it behind."

The truck is already full. Mesfin climbs on first, then holds out his hand to me. Together we pull Shewit and Almaz up. Bodies press against me from all sides. It's hot, and the sun beats down relentlessly. Almaz and I push our way farther into the truck, but there is no room to sit.

The smugglers jump up and find a place to sit at the edge, resting their rifles on their knees. Shewit and Mesfin also find a place along the truck's edge, where it's cooler and less squashed. Before we can push our way back over to them, the engine revs loudly and we move slowly toward the desert in a haze of dust and diesel fumes.

We drive for hours without stopping. Although we speak different languages, I still manage to work out that the other people on the truck have come from the refugee camp farther south. They had been driving for an hour when they reached our town. There are a few boys my age, older men, and also a woman with a boy younger than Lemlem.

My mouth is so dry that it's painful to swallow. My eyes are sore. As the reddish mountains and the town melt into the distance, a flat yellow landscape sprawls out around us in every direction. I feel as if I am speeding toward my future in a billowing cloud of orange sand.

Almaz turns and smiles.

I know why she is smiling. It's good to feel part of something again. Part of a group. It makes our journey seem almost normal. I smile back.

"Ato Medhanie must make a lot of money," I say.

# Desert 2

For four days we drive, stopping only once in the morning and once in the afternoon to eat bread and cold lentils and to drink water. Then the stew runs out and we have only hard bread. At night we sleep under tattered plastic sheets, Almaz between her parents and me next to Mesfin. We dig a shallow pit in the sand and place the sheets on top, weighed down around the edges with another layer of sand. There are six or seven other people sharing our pit each evening. I can start to see my ribs again. As the road changes from gritty track to no road at all, we move more slowly, often sliding through soft sand, steering toward some point that only the driver magically knows. Sometimes I see a plume of dust in the distance. Maybe another truck bumping across the desert to the border.

Our ears become so accustomed to the rumble of the engine that there is a constant ringing noise in them when we stop. While we drive, Almaz and I get used to speaking loudly and lip-reading to understand. Almaz stares at me intently to make sure she doesn't miss anything I am saying. She always pauses before answering, careful not to waste words. It's exhausting to talk for long. We mostly discuss where we want to live in England.

"A big city," says Almaz. "A big city will have good movie theaters and music. My mother knows some people in London."

"I don't know much about England," I confess. "My uncle has a friend in London, too. My mother knows somebody in the north. I don't know where. I think it's cold in the north, though."

"I heard it's cold everywhere," she says. "It's like rainy season all the time."

"But there must be a dry season, too."

I think about Mom and Lemlem back at home. Who will I live with, without my family? It might take Mom a lot longer than six months to be able to leave now that the military is watching her. I want to stay with Almaz, Shewit, and Mesfin. Perhaps they won't want me with them once we arrive in England. They will be busy looking for jobs and looking for a school for Almaz. I would be one extra person to think about.

The truck labors through a ridge of soft sand. As it nears the top, we slow despite the whining revs of the engine. Diesel fumes drift over the trailer and we slide to a stop. I hear the driver's door open and he jumps down into the sand, shouting up to the men with guns.

One of the smugglers near the footboard shouts back angrily. "Everyone off!" he orders.

Our legs are stiff from lack of use. Slowly we climb down onto the footboard, then jump into the hot sand. Almaz and I wade toward her parents, who are waiting in the desert, several yards from the truck.

"Are you okay, Mom?" Almaz asks.

"A little thirsty," she answers, "but at least we had a place to sit." Shewit unwinds the scarf from her head. "Come." She points to the sand, intending to shade us all with her scarf.

Before I can join them, one of the smugglers points at me and shouts, "You!"

On the sand in front of him lies a pile of shovels. He chooses nine or ten other men and directs us each to a wheel. A different smuggler orders us to collect some worn wooden planks from the floor of the trailer.

Without the breeze we enjoyed while driving, the pounding sun from above and the heat rising from the sand below start to seep through my skin, claiming me piece by piece for the parched desert. I blink the sweat from my eyes and try to breathe steadily.

For an hour we dig away sand and place planks in front of the wheels, until the truck has inched to the top of the dune. The driver gets out to look for the firmest route down.

My head is swimming and the blood thumps in my temples.

"We need water," one of the other men says in English.

One of the smugglers slings his rifle over his shoulder and unties a yellow water container from

the side of the truck. He pours a small plastic cup-
ful for each of the men who helped dig out the truck.
Then half a cup for the passengers strewn around the
truck. They scramble to their feet and form an anx-
ious line, but no one pushes. They let the family with
the young boy move to the front.

The truck engine revs again and slides down the
dune toward firmer sand. People walk slowly after
it. Shewit grabs my hands and looks at them, tutting
and shaking her head when she sees the raw blisters,
which sting from my salty sweat. At least the sweat
might stop them from getting infected. There is no
spare water to wash away the dirt.

Almaz and I climb back into the truck. I hold out
my hand to Shewit and Mesfin, then take up my spot
in the middle.

"Thank you for digging us out," says Almaz while
we can still hear each other.

With barely enough energy to keep myself upright,
I smile back.

The truck sets off, creating a wonderful warm
wind, and we rumble on toward the glow of the setting sun on the horizon.

# Desert 3

The next morning, I am stiff from digging, and cold. A feeling I try to savor. We roll up the plastic sheets and set off while the sun is still a thin line in the distance. Medhanie said it would take five days to cross the desert. Maybe tonight we will reach the border.

After several hours, the flat desert rises up into small rocky hills ahead. The truck begins to rattle more than usual as the ground beneath becomes harder, with only a thin layer of soft sand on top.

There is a sudden bang, and the truck jumps as if

it's been bitten, flinging the passengers sitting along the edge off the truck and onto the gritty track. They land with sickening thumps. There is the smell of diesel and the vehicle leans drunkenly. Almaz clings to me as we are crushed by the weight of people sliding to one side of the trailer. The pressure lifts as they start to scramble over the side and backboards and jump to the ground. People begin shouting and wailing. We can't see what is happening.

I hold Almaz by the shoulders and look in her eyes. "Are you hurt?"

"Yes, my arm, but I think it's only bruised. You?"

"I'm okay. Let's find your parents."

We clamber up to the side and jump down to join the other passengers gathering in groups around people lying on the ground. The front wheel of the truck is bent to one side, next to a large rock.

The driver is sitting on the ground with blood running down his face.

One of the armed men is shouting into his mobile phone.

"I can't see Mom and Dad," says Almaz.

She starts running among the injured. Some are

crying out, or clutching their arms or legs. Five or six aren't moving.

Almaz spots her father. He is kneeling in the sand, bent over someone. She rushes to his side and I see that Shewit is lying in front of him. Almaz brings her hands to her mouth and lets out a small cry. I follow her to Mesfin's side.

"Get water," he says calmly.

I run back through the sand to the truck and tug at one of the yellow containers until it comes loose. In the confusion, the smugglers don't see me. There is a little water left at the bottom.

When I return, Shewit's eyes are open. "My leg. What has happened to my leg?"

I look down and see that below the knee her leg is bent at an unnatural angle. "I think your leg is broken," I say.

"I'm so thirsty," Shewit replies.

I pour a little water into the lid of the container and pass it to Almaz. She gently tips it into her mother's mouth. The sun is fierce, and Almaz removes her headscarf to make some shade for her mother.

There is a man who seems to be a doctor, walking

among the people lying on the ground. He crouches down next to Shewit. He looks as if he's Mesfin's age, but with many more wrinkles around his eyes.

"Does it hurt anywhere apart from your leg?" he asks.

"No, just my leg."

He lifts the fabric toward Shewit's knee and she cries out. "You're lucky it's not your femur, but you have a nasty fracture in your lower leg. I have to put a splint on it to hold the bone in place until you can get to the hospital."

Almaz looks up and catches my eye.

"Do you know how far we are from the border?" I ask.

He shakes his head. "We need something to use as a splint."

I look around and see several bundles of firewood hanging from the back of the truck. I pull out one long piece and take it back to the doctor.

"That will work," he says, snapping the stick in two. "Can I rip your dress?" He tears some fabric from the bottom of Shewit's dress, then rips it into smaller pieces. One piece he gives to Shewit. "Put this between your teeth to bite down on. Hold your daughter's hand. Okay, are you ready?"

He gently places the sticks on either side of the bent bone and begins to push it back into place. Shewit screams with pain, then her eyes close as she passes out.

"It is better that way," the doctor says without looking up.

Tears run down Almaz's face.

Mesfin says nothing. He strokes his wife's forehead.

The doctor finishes securing the splint to Shewit's leg. "This will allow her to travel without causing the fracture to worsen. She needs as much water as you can give her."

He stands up and looks around. People are waving at him and shouting to get his attention.

One of the smugglers fires a shot in the air. There is silence, only the sound of one woman moaning in pain, as everyone who can turns to look at the man with the gun. He starts shouting, but I can only understand a few words of what he says.

Almaz is listening intently. As soon as he finishes

talking, people start gathering the items scattered around the truck.

"He says that we're close to the border, only ten miles away," Almaz says. Two large tears spill down her face; she wipes them away. "He says we have to walk. We should reach the border by nightfall, when another truck will come to collect us. They'll send a smaller truck into the desert tomorrow for the wounded and take them to be treated."

I hear the man with the gun shouting again. I think he is trying to get people moving.

Mesfin speaks again. "Almaz, shikorina, your mother cannot walk. We have to rest here and leave tomorrow when the other truck comes. You must go ahead with Shif. You must not miss the boat."

"No!" It is the first time I have ever heard Almaz raise her voice. "I'm staying here with you and Mom. You'll need me to help you carry her and look after her."

"I can look after your mother."

"I won't go without you."

My last night at home comes rushing back to me. The feeling of emptiness when Mom told me that she and Lemlem wouldn't be coming with me.

"You must go ahead. I have to wait for your mother's leg to heal before they'll let her travel on the boat. I've already paid for our crossing and I won't get the money back. It will be your job to get in touch with Aunty in England so when your mother and I reach the port, she can wire enough money for us to take the boat. If you don't go now, we'll all be stuck here. We have our mobile phone. When we get to somewhere where I can buy a SIM card, then I'll call Aunty with our new number. You will know where we are."

Almaz buries her face in her hands.

Mesfin looks at me. "Take care of my daughter. That is your job from this minute onward. I know that I can trust you with her life—you've saved it once already."

I nod, but I don't know if he is right to trust me with anyone's life.

Shewit begins to stir and moan. Mesfin lifts the lid with water to her lips. Behind us, those who can still walk have gathered their few belongings together and are waiting next to the smugglers, trying to shelter in the shade of the truck. The smugglers pass water containers to the men. Only a few containers are left.

"Let's move Mom to the shade," says Almaz.

Mesfin lifts Shewit under the shoulder, and Almaz and I slide our arms under her thighs to support her.

She cries out in pain. "Please, please leave me here."

We walk crabwise as fast as we can to the shade by the truck. Shewit is moaning in agony when we rest her in the sand.

I spot our laundry bag marooned on the ground nearby. I drag it over to Shewit and Mesfin.

"You keep this," I say. "You might need extra clothes to keep warm at night."

The smuggler shouts something else I don't understand, but he stands up, and the people scattered around him get slowly to their feet.

I say good-bye to Mesfin and Shewit. Almaz hugs her father, then bends down to kiss her mother on the cheek. Shewit is barely conscious.

"I will see you soon, Mom," Almaz whispers.

Then Almaz stands up and walks with me toward the man with the gun. Tears stream down her face. Mine, too.

While other passengers sift through the precious objects in their bags to see if there is something they can leave behind, it seems Almaz and I are shedding family and friends as we make our way north.

Although the midday sun is beating down, we begin to walk slowly through the stony sand, our feet slipping back with each step.

After two hours we stop for water. Each person is allowed one capful from the container. There is no more food. My feet are blistered from the sand and sweat rubbing inside my shoes. My hands sting. My head thumps to the rhythm of my heartbeat; my body is so hot that everything feels swollen.

Almaz struggles to keep up with the pace set by the smugglers. She isn't alone. Several people begin to fall behind, including the family with the small boy. I hold out my hand to Almaz.

"It's easier to walk when I have both hands free," she says without stopping.

The group that started out together from the damaged truck is scattered across the desert behind us, moving so slowly that it's hard to tell the people from the rocks that are forever lodged within the shifting sands.

My thoughts are strangely calm. I don't have spare energy to focus on anything but placing one foot in front of the other. I hope that Almaz is feeling a similar temporary peace.

As the sun begins to drift down toward the horizon, I see the outline of a truck several hundred feet ahead. One of the smugglers shouts something, and a man on the truck shouts back. He waves his gun in the air. We have to hurry up. Five or six men with guns are waiting for us.

Perhaps fifty people gather around the armed men. I cannot see the family with the young boy. They start to herd us up onto the back of the truck.

Almaz touches my arm. "Please come with me," she says. "I don't want to speak to them on my own." She walks toward one of the armed men. "When will the truck come to pick up the people who are hurt?" she asks in English.

Without turning round, he grunts a single word at her.

She turns to me. "He says tomorrow." Almaz seems reassured but asks me, "Do you think they have enough water to last them until tomorrow?"

"They left some containers with the injured people. Your mom and dad are sensible. They'll stay in the shade, and they won't be walking, which is what uses up water."

We are the last to climb up, and we sit right at the back. I wrap one arm underneath one of the water canisters and hold on to Almaz's arm with the other. The engine sounds ridiculously loud as it revs in the descending darkness. We lurch slowly through the sand, rocking a little from side to side as the wheels struggle to grip. This truck is smaller than the first one and even more cramped, though there are fewer of us.

Almaz dozes on my shoulder. My eyes ache with exhaustion. I promised to look after her and I know that if she slips off the back while she sleeps, they won't even notice. And if they do, they won't stop the truck to go and look for her. Apart from my family, Almaz is the most precious thing I have. I will not let her go.

# Near and Far

At dawn I see what looks like a large town ahead. The truck leaves the wide road and starts whining down narrower streets lined with square white buildings. There is a new smell in the air, a bit like when my mother cooks alicha. Birds circle and screech overhead.

"We're near the sea," says Almaz. "You can smell the seaweed. It smells a little bit like cabbage."

"How do you know? Have you been to the ocean before?" I ask her.

"One of my father's sisters lives near the coast.

We went to visit her once when I was little. The water was warm and some people were swimming. I don't remember it very well, but I do remember the smell."

I can tell that she is thinking about her parents. I want to distract her somehow.

"England is an island, so we'll never be far from the ocean there. Maybe we could go together," I say.

The truck slows and pulls over at the side of a narrow road. One of the smugglers starts tapping people on the shoulder and gesturing that they should get out. He taps me and Almaz. Soon there are about fifteen of us standing on the sidewalk, wrapping our arms around ourselves against the cold morning breeze.

We follow the smuggler through the doors to one of the accommodation blocks and into a small room on the third floor.

"Here you will wait for the boat," he says in English. "But first we'll check your money."

As we sit on the floor, silent tears roll down Almaz's cheek. Her shoulders begin to shake and through a sob she says, "How will Mom and Dad find me in England?"

"You know the same phone numbers, so you'll be looking for the same people. Your dad said you should get in touch with your aunty, and your parents will be in touch with her, too, so she can send them money. When they come, they will find you. Don't worry. At least they aren't too far behind you." I realize that I sound confident, reassuring. Not like myself.

The smugglers didn't wait for the slower walkers to reach the new truck. So I know they won't send a truck for the injured passengers. There would be no extra money, and they would be responsible for a truckful of injured people. But I have learned that sometimes hope itself is as important as the thing you are actually hoping for.

The smuggler writes all our names down, which takes a long time as we speak several languages among us. He asks in English if we have paid or not.

"You must be quiet," he says before he leaves. He taps his gun and points to the door. Men with guns will be waiting outside. I wonder how the money my uncle wired to the man in the white shirt could have made it up here.

An hour or so later the man returns. He walks over

to a lady by the window, which has a sheet draped in front of it.

"You need to pay one thousand, six hundred dollars," he says.

She looks up at him and shouts something back—not in English.

"Quiet," he snaps, but she stands up and starts waving her arms, still shouting.

The man grabs her by the arm and drags her toward the door. I hear screaming and shouting in the corridor, and a loud cracking sound, then she is quiet.

Almaz grips my arm.

After a few minutes he returns. This time he goes over to one of the men in our group. "You also need to pay one thousand, six hundred dollars."

The man replies in his own language, but quietly. Eventually he takes a phone offered by the man with the gun. He is calling a friend or a relative. Maybe they will have the money, but if not, the man will be staying here.

The smuggler turns and looks at me and Almaz but doesn't come over.

For three days we wait in the room. I am used to small spaces now, but some of the others pace around and shout at the smugglers until they come into the room and threaten to take them away. But we are given hot food to eat and warm blankets to sleep on. There is even a toilet in the corridor outside.

We can hear the sea at night. It's maybe a tenth of a mile from our room. I wish that Mom and Lemlem were waiting with me. Lemlem would sit on my lap and Mom would talk to me about what kind of work she might get, about whether we might live near the sea. She would wonder if the injera will be any good.

To pass the time, Almaz teaches me what she knows about dinosaurs. We invent a stupid game, where she tells me the name of a dinosaur and I have to guess what it looks like. I get *T. rex* right, but apart from that I have to accept it's really not a strong subject for me. In return, I try to teach her how to play chess; how to set up the board, and what the different pieces are called. I realize it sounds like a ridiculous game unless you've actually seen a chessboard in action.

We are both exhausted from the desert journey, and the rest of the time we doze. Almaz rests her head on my lap rather than the hard floor, and I lean against the wall. A few months ago I could never have imagined a girl sleeping on my lap, but here it feels completely normal.

In the middle of the night, after the third day, there is a knock on the door. Three smugglers come in.

"Boat," says one of them in English. "Put on all your clothes and come."

Almaz and I are already wearing everything we own.

We walk sleepily down the stairs to a truck waiting outside. A cool wind is blowing in from the ocean and seeps through my thin layers of clothing in a few seconds.

We climb into the truck and the man gestures that we should move into the middle, as close together as possible. Once we are squashed into a tiny space, one of the armed men climbs in. The others begin passing him huge sacks, which he stacks around us. The sacks of rice are a decoy. In the middle of them sits the true cargo: people.

Soon we are completely hidden behind a wall of rice. The sacks push down on us, shunting us farther into the middle of the truck. At least they protect us from the freezing morning air, but I don't know for how long we will be traveling like this.

The truck bumps slowly along the road, and after a few minutes we must join a highway of some kind. The truck chugs along at top speed. After a little while I drift off to sleep.

I wake maybe several hours later. We have stopped, and the smugglers are throwing bread rolls and bottles of water into the truck. Then we keep going. We must be traveling along the coastline. The wind is still strong, but doesn't drive away the gathering clouds. I can hear seabirds screeching over the roar of the engine.

By late afternoon, the truck comes to a stop again. This time we climb out and gather next to a strip of sandy beach with a small concrete jetty jutting into the shallow sea. I have never seen the sea before. Almaz is staring out across the water. The horizon is gray, which makes the water seem dark blue, almost black.

Gathered around the jetty are men clutching bright-orange jackets. They walk toward us, waving the orange bundles at us and talking urgently.

"Who wants to buy a life jacket?" asks one of the smugglers.

Almaz and I have no money, but some people in our group are reaching into their pockets.

"Do you think we need one?" Almaz asks, looking concerned.

"No, we have a boat. We don't need a life jacket, too."

Almaz looks up at me and smiles her warm smile, which helps me to forget the biting wind for a moment.

The smuggler points to two small orange inflatable dinghies. I look at them in horror.

He sees my face and says, "No, no. Big boat." He points out to sea.

We are to get in the little boats, which will take us to a bigger boat.

"Do you think there really is a bigger boat?" Almaz whispers.

"I guess if there were lots of little boats, then they would need to pay lots of people to sail them. It makes more sense for them to use one big boat," I whisper back.

The smugglers point to me and the other men, and we start to drag one of the boats toward the edge of the water. We push it alongside the narrow jetty until it begins to bob up and down by itself. We push the second boat up behind it. The smugglers herd the others onto the jetty, but I can't see Almaz. For a second I panic and then realize she is in the middle of the group of women. I push my way past the men, and even though one of the smugglers is shouting at me, I go and stand with Almaz.

People begin to step gingerly into the nearest boat. It wobbles and they sit down abruptly. When there are seven or eight people sitting down, the guard nods to Almaz, who steps into the middle of the second boat. I follow. The smuggler tips the engine propeller down into the water and tugs at the starter cord. A high-pitched roar breaks the silence and we steer slowly away from the jetty.

Almaz shivers in the breeze and spray flicks up onto our thin clothes, sucking away any warmth we have left. I put my arm around her shoulder, and it steadies us both as waves slam against the bottom of the boat. As we carve a path out to sea, I decide that I don't like being surrounded by water. It seems alive; it seems angry.

After a few minutes the smuggler at the back of the boat shouts and points. In front I see a large blue fishing boat bobbing on the water. Almaz looks up at me, and I smile, full of relief that there is a big boat after all.

We must be the last people to join. As we steer closer, I can see hundreds of heads, moving up and down as the boat gently rocks with the waves.

We pull up to where a rope ladder hangs over the side of the larger boat. Our dinghy is moving to a different rhythm in the waves, and the boats bump against each other.

Men wait at the top, their arms outstretched. Almaz tries to grip the rope without falling between the two boats. She clings on, and looks up, reaching a hand to the next rung, where one of the men grabs her arm and begins to haul her toward the top. The other women go next; then it's my turn.

As I jump into the hull of the bigger blue boat, I

feel safer. Next to me is a mother with a small baby strapped to her chest in layers of bright cloth. The wooden sides and gentler motion are reassuring. Almaz pushes through the closely packed bodies to reach me. I think we are lucky to be near the edge. From the middle of the boat wafts a sour smell of vomit. Not everyone is okay with the rolling of the waves. Lots of people are wearing the bright life jackets they were selling by the jetty. They look warmer than everyone else. There is no roof or shelter from the wind, and although it's not yet dusk, the clouds make it feel later.

There is a grating vibration through the floor of the boat as they haul in the anchor. I guess that's what's happening because right after that, the boat spins around, and we start bumping through the waves toward Europe.

Almaz and I have been thrown together once more with people we know nothing of. Only, this time there has been no time to talk, no chance to learn anything of the lives that brought the others to share this boat with us. Are they scared, too? There is no one to turn to for reassurance. Then, as I look up, I recognize the doctor, separated from us by two or three rows of people. He must have stayed in a different safe house.

"Hey, Doctor!" I shout. The words leave my mouth before I have a chance to stop them.

He turns around, as do many others to see who is making the noise. He nods at me and shouts hello.

It is a small thing, but I feel better. Safer. I feel Almaz slip her hand inside mine. I feel a flicker of warmth as I realize that she has no doubts about me; she trusts me to look after her.

We haven't been sailing for very long when the wind becomes much stronger and the clouds lower. The engine of the boat splutters as we ride the waves, struggling under its heavy load. I can hear the men steering the boat shouting to one another. The first few drops of rain begin to fall, and I put my arm around Almaz's shoulder again. We are both shivering, our faces shiny wet with spray and rainwater.

I don't know if the sea is always this rough. I see my fear reflected in the faces surrounding us.

# Boat

Cold salty water stings my eyes and soaks my T-shirt. I cling to the clammy wooden edge of the boat as a huge wave swells toward me. The boat tips, and I gasp as people slide against me and the air is pressed from my chest.

The sky is turning from light to dark gray; white foam tops the waves. The wind pushes relentlessly against my face, and with the next rolling wave the boat dips so low that buckets of water gush in over the side, soaking me again with freezing water. I feel it creeping above my ankles. No one cries out.

Even the baby strapped to the mother beside me is quiet.

Green-gray waves make a wall around us. We rise to the top of another but there is nothing to see except spray blowing like rain in the icy wind. Europe is sprawled somewhere in front of us but I can't see land. As we slide into the trough, more water rushes over the side of the boat. It's up to my knees. My feet are numb but I can tell that my shoes are heavy with water. I look up again and see a swirling wave bigger than the others rolling toward us in fury. The boat tips. This time we keep on tipping. The wave crashes over us as if we are on the shore, only we're in the middle of the sea. I hear screaming and then nothing as water rushes over my head.

I can't tell which way is up to sky and wind, and which way is down toward the depths of sea beneath. I open my eyes. They sting but show me nothing more than cloudy bubbling water and the legs of someone just out of reach. I kick up once, my chest burning. I kick up again, knowing that in a second I'll no longer be able to fight the desperate urge to breathe in. I kick one last time, my legs tingling. I am about to pass out just as wind blasts my face; I suck in air and some spray.

Choking, I pant and gasp; the currents tug me left and right as the swell lifts me up and down. I cannot swim but instinct makes me kick my feet to stay afloat. The shoes my mother bought with three weeks' wages are so heavy. I try to push them off without going under.

I know I can't kick water for long. Already my thighs and arms feel tired. I see four, maybe five, other heads swirling in the waves. How can three hundred people disappear so quickly?

A yellow plastic bag washes toward me. There are clothes inside. The knot has been tied tightly so the bag is like a floating pocket of air. I cling to it.

A boy appears next to me, bobbing up from under the waves like I did seconds before. I reach out my hand to him. He looks at me. His eyes are big and oval-shaped and he reminds me of Bini. I reach my hand out to him again and he tries to grab it but instead sinks beneath the waves. He doesn't come back up.

Who will come to save me? Who knows where I

am apart from the others tossing and bobbing in the waves like me? What would Bini do now?

As the next wave lifts me up, I see Almaz clinging to a yellow container. I lose sight of her in the spray but the container is bright and I fix my eyes on it with absolute determination. Slowly I kick my legs, which does nothing, but the waves are moving us together. As she drifts closer, she turns and sees me. She reaches out a hand. I stretch mine and grab her fingertips, then her wrist. We cling to each other, with the container and bag to keep us afloat.

Our lives depend on a plastic bag and a water container.

Almaz's lips are blue and her hands keep slipping from the container.

"Kick water!" I shout.

I put my hands over the top of hers and press down on the yellow plastic.

I become aware of a new sound over the roar of the wind and waves. It is coming from overhead. The sea around me flattens in a circle of white spray, as if pushed by a great wind from above. I look up and see an orange figure slicing through the sky toward me. Above the figure a red-and-white helicopter hovers.

I look down at Almaz, but she is no longer clinging to the yellow water container. I turn frantically around, the seawater streaming down my face. I cannot see her anywhere. Her hands must have slipped from beneath mine, my fingers so numb I didn't notice. She has gone.

I feel something touch my leg and plunge my head beneath the waves, reaching my arms downward. I grab some clothes and, with my muscles burning, pull upward. There is an arm, and I tug it toward my chest, dragging the rest of the body with me to the surface. Almaz's whole face is bluish.

The orange figure is next to me and clips something to me. Then they clip something to Almaz. We are flying up through the air toward the helicopter. The orange figure pats me on the back.

We reach the helicopter's mouth and strong arms pull us in toward the center. They strap me into a seat in the corner, then turn immediately to Almaz. One person holds her wrist; another sweeps their fingers inside her mouth. They place a mask over her nose and mouth. It's attached to a small bag, which one of them squeezes, while the other presses down on the mask. Almaz coughs and they push her to sit upright; she coughs more and some water comes out. They lay her on her side. Her eyes flicker open and look at my bare feet.

I sit back in my seat and close my eyes as someone pushes a bottle of water into my hand. I can barely grip it. My body feels so heavy; my legs and arms ache as if they have been bruised all over. But I don't care.

Almaz nearly sank beneath the waves, like so many others, but now she is lying here, next to me, alive.

We have the chance for a second life.

Inside my head I carry the stories of what went before. Those stories are the threads that will tie me to my other life. I am still Shif. But from now on there will always be two parts to me.

I hope the people I love can join me and Almaz soon. Then the raw edges of my divided world can begin to heal. In the meantime, we have each other.

# Author's note

I began writing *Refugee 87* when I was living far from home with my family, in Ethiopia. Our move to Africa coincided with the height of a global refugee crisis. News channels showed images of refugees fleeing war or persecution in their own countries. Some of these people were from Ethiopia.

Everyone I knew back in the UK was shocked by the images of refugees on the news, but many didn't know why people were risking their lives in this way. The more I heard the phrase "boatload" of refugees, or people discussed in terms of quantity, the more I wanted to hear about *who* these people were, and what they might be escaping from. People don't make perilous journeys unless they are leaving something worse behind.

While we were in Ethiopia, a state of emergency was declared after anti-government riots. We were on lockdown in the capital, Addis Ababa, for a few weeks. The internet was shut down, as well as the phones briefly. New laws said you could be put in jail just for criticizing the government. There were systems in place to help us leave the city—and country—if we needed to, but the experience changed me. Why should I be able to leave easily if I was in danger, but not my Ethiopian friends?

Before moving to Ethiopia, I was, for many years, a children's book editor. I'd often spoken to authors about their inspirations, but I'd never planned to have any of my own. Now there was a story I wanted to tell. The story of a boy who had left everything he knew in search of safety. That story was *Refugee 87*. For the first time, I truly understood the need to write.

I immediately knew where the book would be set. I also decided not to name the country where Shif comes from, or any of the countries he passes through. I wanted the focus to be on his experience rather than the politics of one regime. Also, Shif's story has echoes for children across the world today—Central America, Syria, Myanmar, South Sudan. I have left many clues in the story, though, if the reader wants to find out. All the places exist, and Shif's journey can be traced on a map from beginning to end.

Debra Hurford-Brown

# About the Author

**Ele Fountain** worked as an editor in children's publishing, where she was responsible for launching and nurturing the careers of many award-winning and bestselling authors. She lived in Addis Ababa, Ethiopia, for several years, where she was inspired to write *Refugee 87*, her debut novel. Ele now lives in what she describes as a "not quite falling-down house" south of London with her husband and two young daughters.